MISSISSIPPI TRIAL, 1955

Chris Crowe

D0193405

speak
An Imprint of Penguin Group (USA) Inc.

SPEAK

Published by Penguin Group

Penguin Group (USA) Inc.,

345 Hudson Street, New York, New York 10014, U.S.A.

Penguin Books Ltd, 80 Strand, London WC2R ORL, England

Penguin Books Australia Ltd, 250 Camberwell Road,
Camberwell, Victoria 3124, Australia

Penguin Books Canada Ltd, 10 Alcorn Avenue,
Toronto, Ontario, Canada M4V 3B2

Penguin Books (N.Z.) Ltd, 182-190 Wairau Road,
Auckland 10, New Zealand

First published in the United States of America by Phyllis Fogelman
Books, an imprint of Penguin Putnam Inc., 2002
Published by Speak, an imprint of Penguin Group (USA) Inc., 2003

20 19 18 17 16 15 14 13 12 11

THE LIBRARY OF CONGRESS HAS CATALOGED
THE PHYLLIS FOGELMAN EDITION AS FOLLOWS:

Crowe, Chris.

Mississippi trial, 1955 / by Chris Crowe.

p. cm.

Summary: In Mississippi in 1955, a white sixteen-year-old finds himself at
odds with his grandfather over issues surrounding the kidnapping and
murder of a fourteen-year-old African American from Chicago.

ISBN: 0-8037-2745-3 (hc)

[1. Grandfathers—Fiction. 2. Fathers and sons—Fiction. 3. Racism—Fiction.
4. Till, Emmett, 1941–1955—Fiction. 5. African Americans—Mississippi—
Fiction. 6. Mississippi—Race relations—Fiction.] I. Title.

PZ7.C8853845 Mi 2002   [Fic]—dc21   2001040221

Speak ISBN 0-14-250192-1

Printed in the United States of America

For my parents,
Ruth Anne and Richard E. Crowe

CHAPTER 1

My dad hates hate.

All my life, if the word ever slipped out of my mouth, he'd snap into me faster than a rattlesnake.

"Hiram," he'd say, straightening up tall like a preacher, "the world's got plenty enough hate without you adding to it. I will not tolerate such language—or even such thinking—in my home or in my family!" He'd go on with his sermon for too long, five minutes or more, preaching about the evils of hate and reminding me how hate had hurt folks back in our old home, the Mississippi Delta. Then he'd march me up to the bathroom and give my tongue a slathering of Lifebuoy soap.

I can't tell you which was worse, the sermons or the soap, but I will tell you this: I hated Dad when he acted like that, like some kind of born-again crusader out to protect everybody's right to life, liberty, and the pursuit of happiness.

By the time I turned sixteen last July, I'd had it with Dad's sermons and weirdness about hate, racism, equal rights, and all that. Funny thing was, the more he preached about hate, the madder it made me. Never told him to his face, of course. It wouldn't have been worth it, but I let him know in a thousand ways that I'd just as soon live in the Arizona desert with Gila monsters and tarantulas than spend any time with him.

But a few months ago, the summer of 1955, lots of stuff happened, stuff I never would have imagined. It was strange, but you know how sometimes when you get what you think you always wanted, it turns out to be nothing like you expected?

That happened to me when I was back in Greenwood, Mississippi, last summer. Some awful things happened to a Negro kid named Emmett Till, and I was right in the middle of it, smack in the heart of crazy, senseless hatred. And you know what? When it was all over, I started seeing Dad—and lots of people—a whole lot different than ever before.

I first started butting heads with Dad in 1948—I was only nine—because he dragged us away from Mississippi. Dad and his dad, Grampa Hillburn, got along about as well as Hitler and Roosevelt. Spend any time with the two of them in the same room, and you'd figure that World War II hadn't ended yet. The problem was that while Dad was away fighting Japanese in the Pacific and Mom was working for the war effort, Gramma and Grampa Hillburn raised me. They spoiled me pretty good, I guess, but as a little kid, I liked the spoiling, and I loved my grandparents. And their big old house. And Greenwood, Mississippi.

Dad came home from the war, took one look at how tight I was with Grampa, another look at the South he hated, and used the GI Bill to go up to Ole Miss to get a master's degree in English so he could land a college teaching job out west, far away from Grampa, from Mississippi, from racism and prejudice, from hate. Mom and Dad lived in a shoe box–size apartment up there, so while Dad studied and Mom worked at Oxford Elementary School, they let me stay with Gramma and Grampa for the two years it took Dad to finish school.

Looking back on it now, I can see how lots of things that happened when I used to live in Greenwood stacked up to set the stage for all the horrible stuff that took place last summer.

I still remember being a little kid in Greenwood. I spent nearly all my time with Grampa, and we had a regular routine: After breakfast we'd walk down to the Leflore County Courthouse so Grampa could "do a little business." That usually meant he'd stroll into someone's office, pull up a chair, and visit. Usually, before he'd even sit down, he'd fish in his pocket for a nickel, hand it to me, and say, "Hiram, Mr. Hardin and I have some serious business to tend to for the next little while. Why don't you run down to the lobby and see what Mr. Paul's got for sale today."

Funny how you remember some days more than others, but I still remember one summer morning there. With the nickel in my fist, I left Mr. Hardin's office and headed straight for the glass cases and counters in the center hall-way of the courthouse.

"Hey, Mr. Paul, it's me, Hiram Hillburn."

"Little Hiram, how's the world treating you this morning?" Mr. Paul turned to face me, smiling with his hands flat on the glass countertops. He looked about my dad's age, and I knew he'd been in the war too. His Army truck hit a land mine in France and he ended up blind. Dark glasses hid his eyes.

"Grampa gave me a nickel."

"That right? Nobody can say old Earl Hillburn doesn't know how to occupy his grandchild. What'll it be today, Hiram?"

I walked up to the glass display cases and looked over the rows of gum and candy bars laid out on the shelves. Behind the counter, Mr. Paul kept an ice chest full of soda, and on the right side of the display case he kept a cooler filled with ice cream bars. It was a hard decision.

"I've got some cold Co'-Cola back here," he said, "but I know you like those Eskimo Pies too."

This particular morning was cooler than most summer mornings had been, so I had my eye on something else.

"Could I please have a Hershey's bar, Mr. Paul?"

Keeping his head upright, he reached carefully into the display case and felt around until his hand found the dark brown Hershey's bars. He set one on the counter. "That'll be five cents."

I snapped my nickel flat on the glass top. Mr. Paul felt for it, picked it up, and dropped it into the cigar box he kept on a shelf behind him. "Pleasure doing business with you, Hiram. What big things do you and your grampa have planned for today?"

"Dunno, sir." I peeled the wrapper off my chocolate bar and broke off a section. "He'll probably be talking in there with Mr. Hardin for a while longer. Then we'll go out to the fields and work some before lunch."

Mr. Paul grinned. "Work? You mean your grampa will drive out there and watch those boys sweating in his fields while he sits in his truck drinking lemonade and reading the paper. I'd surely like to get some of that kind of work for myself." A man approached the counter, and, hearing him, Mr. Paul said, "Well, I've got to get back to business. You have yourself a good day, Hiram, and stay out of the way of that busy grampa of yours."

I meandered down the marble hallway and out the main courthouse doors. A huge magnolia tree shaded the front of the building, and I walked under the tree and pulled myself up into its lowest branches, resting comfortably in a shady nook to enjoy my candy bar and wait for Grampa.

When Grampa came out of the courthouse, we walked back home, got into his pickup, and drove north of Greenwood for a few miles on Old Money Road, past flat wide fields furrowed with dark green cotton plants. Once we got to his fields, Grampa parked the truck and turned me loose while he talked with the workers and looked over the crops. I wandered up and down the cotton rows looking for arrowheads or lost tools or anything I could find in the furrows. Grampa always rewarded me with a nickel when I found something. I liked exploring the rows of plants—they offered some shade from the Mississippi sun, and if the wind blew even a little, the plants swayed and stirred up air that seemed almost cool.

When Grampa was done in one part of the field, he'd whistle for me, and we'd drive to the next section. The only person he ever talked to was the field boss, Mr. Irwin, a red-faced man who wore dark green coveralls. Grampa talked to him and then Mr. Irwin told the field hands whatever it was Grampa wanted them to do. They were all colored men; I never saw a white man working Grampa's fields. I hadn't found anything worth a nickel to Grampa, so I followed some of the Negro workers into the rows while they chopped cotton. One man noticed me following behind, and turned to talk to me.

"You Mr. Hillburn's gran'child, ain't you?"

I didn't answer. I was seven years old, and he looked as old as Grampa, and taller. I'd hardly ever talked to a Negro man before, and I was scared.

He smiled and patted me on the head. "'S okay, Little Mr. Hillburn; I was wonderin' why you're followin' me." His deep, gentle voice relaxed me.

"Just watching," I said cautiously. "You choppin' those weeds pretty fast."

"Got to, little man. This whole field needs chopping today, and if we don't finish it, it's gonna be added to tomorrow's work, and if that happens, we ain't never gonna go home tomorrow, and, son, I can't stand the thought of working in this field both day and night."

"I can help. Sometimes I help Gramma in the garden. She says I'm a good worker."

"Bet you are, I bet you are." The man smiled and turned back to his hoeing.

I stepped closer and could see the sweat damp on the back of his shirt. His black forearms, knotted with muscle, gripped the hoe, bringing it up and down rhythmically, knocking out weeds without hurting the cotton plants. I had to almost jog to keep up with him as he swept down the furrows. When we got to the end of the row, Grampa saw us. The Negro worker paused a moment to stand up and stretch his back, and as he did so, I grabbed his hoe and headed back into the cotton.

"Hiram! Hiram Hillburn, you put that down right now!" Grampa shouted. I dropped the hoe and Grampa turned on the worker. "You, boy!" he snapped. "Don't you know any better than to let my grandchild play with that tool? I ain't paying you to be a slacker, so you got no reason to be resting when you should be chopping."

The worker lowered his head.

"Mr. Irwin know you take rests at the end of the row?"

"No, sir," the man replied without looking up.

"I catch you wasting my money again, you'll be working without a lunch break or not working at all. You understand me, boy?"

"Yessir," the man said as he picked up the hoe and turned back to his work.

Grampa often got mad like that: lightning quick, fast and without warning. His voice changed completely, mean: mad and mean at the same time. It scared me. "Hiram, boy, you come here right now."

I trotted to his side but stayed clear of his arm that tried to rest on my shoulders.

"Son, let me tell you something." He patted me on the head. "God made Negroes to work the land. They don't feel the heat like we do; they can work all day long in the most hellish weather. They're strong people, good with their hands."

"I'm good with my hands too, Grampa. Gramma lets me help in the garden."

"Well, sure, you're good with your hands, Hiram, but there's lots more that you can do. These folks, they're doing what the good Lord intended them to do; that don't mean you can't do it too, but you got more in you, boy. You're meant to be the boss, not the worker."

I looked out over the field at the black men, the backs of their shirts stained with sweat, bent over their hoes chopping weeds among the cotton plants. They worked methodically, quickly, almost like machines. I could do that, I thought, but I wouldn't want to do it all day.

I followed Grampa to the truck and climbed into the cab. He handed me a thermos cup of Gramma's cold lemonade. Hot from the time I'd spent in the sun, I gulped it down, no longer thinking about the black men and their backbreaking work out in Grampa's fields.

CHAPTER 2

Coffee. When I was at Gramma and Grampa's house, I woke up every morning to the smell of coffee. The nutty aroma floated up the back stairs and into my room through the transom window above my door. Once I was awake, I tried to separate the other aromas of my grandparents' house: Some mornings the meaty, spicy scent of sausage came up the stairs; other days the sweet fragrance of fresh muffins. Behind those morning smells lingered the mellow scent of mildew, wood, and Ivory soap. To this day, if you dropped me blindfolded at my grandparents' home, I'd know I was there as soon as you opened the door.

Gramma and Grampa lived in a big white two-story house on Market Street, just a block from the Yazoo River and four blocks from the courthouse. Their house looks like a smaller version of the White House in Washington,

D.C., without so many pillars in front and not nearly so tall and wide.

It's the most comfortable place in the world. Gramma had a few wicker chairs out on the front porch and a porch swing to one side. When it was cool enough, we'd sit out there after dinner, but usually Grampa liked sitting in the living room in his big wing-back chair napping or reading the paper. I liked the kitchen best. It's behind the dining room, and you can find your way there by following your nose. Gramma always seemed to have something baking: biscuits, corn bread, cookies, cake, pies. If I wandered in, she'd tell me to sit at the kitchen table while she found me "something suitably sweet to tide you over till supper," and after she set a slice of pie or plate of cookies in front of me, she'd open the icebox and get me a cold drink of milk or lemonade.

The kitchen was a small room with a large window over the sink that looks out onto the Remingtons' backyard. Gramma had a wooden table in the middle of the kitchen where she did most of her "cutting, kneading, and rolling." When it was just Gramma, Grampa, and me for supper, we ate in the kitchen. When Mom or anyone else was there, Gramma insisted we "eat proper in the dining room."

My bedroom, Dad's old room, was directly above the kitchen. It had a squeaky old bed with four high corner posts and a wooden floor that creaked when I walked on it. If I lay quietly on the bed, I could usually hear the muffled clatter of stirring spoons, pots, and pans down in the kitchen. And of course I could always smell what Gramma was cooking.

Evenings Grampa would sit in the wide living room in the front of the house and read *The Greenwood Commonwealth*. He relied on the paper to keep up on the news of his old friends in the South and especially in Greenwood, Mississippi.

"Don't care much for the rest of the world," he told me once. "Didn't like Harlan going off to the Navy. American boys have no business fighting other people's wars. We've got our way of doing things right here, and we've got our own problems to take care of, so it's no kettle of ours if commies or Nazis or anybody else wants to go killing each other. They can rot in Hades for all I care."

I was used to Grampa ranting about things in the paper and I just kept quiet. I'd sit on the floor, looking over the last few days of *The Greenwood Commonwealth*, rereading Li'l Abner and other comics I liked. From the kitchen came the sounds and smells of Gramma cooking. I could hear the sizzle of meat frying on the stove and the open-and-close of the oven as she checked the biscuits or corn bread or pie or whatever she was baking for supper.

One evening, Grampa had been reading the paper for a while. Then he swore and snapped it down on the footstool in front of him. "Hiram, boy, I don't know what this country is coming to. Now the war's over, these damn Yankees are trying to tell us how to run the South. You're still little, but you remember this, son. Our way of life is precious. It's the way I live, the way my daddy lived, my granddaddy, and his daddy before him. It's going to be the way you live too, if I have anything to say about it."

I had no idea what he was talking about, but I didn't say anything because he had that mad look in his eye that he usually had when he argued with Dad. He went on about the South until Gramma called us in for supper.

Gramma could tell Grampa was stirred up about something when she sat down to eat, so before he could even start, she said, "Now, Earl, you remember our rule: No talking politics at the supper table."

"Fine, Florence. I'll just hold all this frustration and nonsense in until tomorrow morning, but don't you go blaming me if I pop open and spray you all like a hot can of beer." His face flushed, and he frowned. Then he looked at me and sighed. "I guess there's no need getting little Hiram all upset. Say the blessing, son, and let's plow into Gramma's supper. And Hiram, ask God Almighty if he might shed a little wisdom on them harebrained Yankees and their Mr. Harry Truman."

After we finished supper, Grampa went back to his paper in the living room, and Gramma started cleaning up. I helped carry the plates and things to the sink, but she shooed me out of the kitchen. "I do appreciate your help, Hiram, but I can manage just fine now. Why don't you go on outside and see if you can find R.C. somewhere."

R. C. Rydell lived way down River Road, along the Yazoo, in a dilapidated old house that he claimed had been in

Greenwood since before the Civil War. At nine, he was two years older than me, but he was one of the few boys my age who always seemed to be outside the same time I was. That night, I swung open the back door and hopped down the steps into the yard. A faint breeze rustled the magnolia tree and azaleas in the backyard, and even though the sun had not yet set, outside was cooler than Gramma's kitchen. I pitched a rock at a stray cat prowling through our bushes. I missed it, but when the rock rustled through the branches, the gray cat dropped low to the ground, arched its back, and hissed. I launched another rock its way.

"Hey, watch what you're doin'!" R.C. stepped through the bushes and into our yard. He had on the same torn and oversized black high-top Keds he always wore. His shirt and jeans were rumpled and dirty, his red hair a tangled mess. He scowled at me like the cat had. "You 'bout put my eye out, Hiram. Ain't your grandaddy taught you 'bout throwin' rocks round people?"

"Sorry, R.C., I was trying to chase that old tomcat out of our yard; he gets into Gramma's garbage cans."

"Ya'll want to be getting rid of a cat, you need a good BB gun, not a rock. A hot BB in the butt'll help that old cat remember to stay out of your yard. I'd borrow you mine, but you're too little to be handlin' a gun."

I'd never seen R.C. with a BB gun, but I didn't question him. He always told more than he had. "So what were you doing up in those bushes?" I asked. "You find a nest or something?"

"Don't you know nothin', Hiram Hillburn? No bird with half a brain would build a nest in a 'zalea bush. Naw, I was just in there so I could get a good look at the Remingtons. They's dancing again."

Ralph and Ronnie Remington lived behind our house. A couple of brothers who had never married, they lived alone in a Southern mansion that probably used to be fancy but was now rundown and surrounded by weeds. R.C. said they were crazy. Grampa said they were addle-brained but harmless. Gramma said they were two lonely old bachelors who drank too much. I'd never spoken to Ralph or Ronnie even though I saw one or the other almost every day. Ralph looked older, his hair had streaks of gray, and he always had a worried look on his face when I'd see him hustling down the sidewalk from downtown with a narrow brown paper bag under his arm. He'd walk down River Road to his house. Then instead of going up the front steps and in the front door, he'd follow a path he'd worn in the grass around the side of the house to the back door.

Ronnie was heavier than Ralph, and his dark hair covered only the sides of his head; Grampa said he looked like a fat monk. He usually wore a baggy Army uniform with no insignias. "Likely he got that uniform from the Salvation Army shop," said Grampa, "because even the U.S. Army knows better than to let a knucklehead like Ronnie anywhere close to their business. If Ronnie Remington'd been in the war, we'd all be speaking German and Japanese right now."

Sometimes I'd see Ronnie down at the courthouse carrying mail and papers from one office to another. Charity work, Grampa called it. Neither of the Remingtons was allowed to drive, so Ronnie walked everywhere in town. He was slow and sort of ambled from one place to another, usually looking for people he knew so he could ask to borrow a nickel. Gramma said he spent all his money on ice cream and cookies, and I guess she was right, because when I saw him strolling home some afternoons, he usually had a small grocery sack clutched to his chest. When Ronnie got near the Remington house, he never walked up the front sidewalk. He had his own path worn through the grass and weeds. It angled from the corner of their yard to the front steps. Funny thing about the Remingtons: Ronnie would only use his path and enter through the front door; Ralph would only use his path and enter through the back.

"Shhh," hissed R.C. "They's dancing. Look." He pointed through an opening in the azaleas that gave us a clear view through one of their back windows. Stripped down to their boxer shorts and tank top undershirts, Ronnie and Ralph waltzed by the window. Before R.C. started giggling, I could hear the faint strains of waltz music from their record player. They passed by again and did a slow, awkward turn in front of the window. While Ralph planted both feet, braced himself, and strained to keep his balance, Ronnie leaned back in a deep dip, letting his thick left arm swing wide and high, his pinky finger extended. Shaking with effort, Ralph managed to pull Ronnie out of the dip and continue their 1-2-3 around the room, and I swear I could hear their floor creaking and sagging. When they came by the window again, I could see Ronnie's sweating face framed in concentration, counting out the waltz steps while Ralph struggled to lead his fat younger brother around the room. They moved like two old cows up on their hind legs.

R.C. could stand it no longer and fell to the ground, snorting and choking, trying to stifle his laughter. "Oh my gawd," he sputtered, "can you believe those two hippos dancing? They oughta put them in the county fair!" He laughed and snorted louder.

"Quiet, R.C.! Dang it, if they hear us, I'm gonna be in big trouble with Gramma. You know she thinks we ought not bother Ralph and Ronnie."

"Quit being a sisbaby. We ain't doing nothing wrong. They's the weirdos dancing around in their underwear."

"Gramma says it's not our business what they do long as they don't bother us. She told me I had to be neighborly and polite and stay out of their way."

R.C. picked up a rock and moved through the azalea bushes toward their house.

"R.C., no!" I hissed as loud as I dared. "We're gonna be in *big* trouble if you do."

Crouched low and partially hidden by the evening's shadows, R.C. wound up and chucked his rock. It cracked against the house just above their window when they waltzed by again. Ralph stumbled and disappeared from view while Ronnie looked pale and stunned for a moment before coming to the window. "What's that? Who's there? You scat now and leave us be. Who's there?"

R.C., still hidden by shadows, let out a loud, low, "Mooaah, mooaah, mooaah, you old cows . . ." and sprinted around their house and down River Road, laughing and mooing all the way.

"Who's there? Who's there?" called out Ronnie nervously. "You just go on and leave us be. Just you scat you and leave us be!"

I ducked back through the bushes and into our yard. Sometimes I didn't like how R.C. played, even if he was older than me. It didn't seem funny at all when Ralph had looked hurtful surprised and Ronnie looked scared.

I trudged up the back steps to the kitchen, hoping Gramma would offer me another slice of apple pie when I got inside.

Maybe that'd get rid of the bad taste in my mouth.

August, a month after my eighth birthday. Grampa and I had been following our summer routine pretty faithfully. Some days, though, I'd stay home and go fishing with R.C. down on the Yazoo. He was a good fisherman even though he always used a cane pole. "I got a nice rod and reel down home, but my daddy don't want me using it without him around. 'Sides, I do just fine with this old cane pole. I bet those fish get scared just knowing I'm coming."

I'd walk the one or two miles out to the edge of town to R.C.'s house, and from there we'd walk a couple miles farther down River Road where the trees and brush cleared away from the riverbanks. Gramma would pack me up a lunch, food enough for two men.

"Gramma," I told her the first time she made the lunch, "you know I don't get that hungry; I don't think I can eat all of this."

"Darling, you never know how hungry fishing might make you; I don't want to be worrying about my only grandson starving down there on the Yazoo. Believe me, it'll all get eaten." She wrapped six gingersnap cookies in wax paper and tucked them into the top of my lunch sack. "When you get to the Rydells' house, you find that little girl Naomi and give these to her. Poor thing probably hasn't had a treat since Christmas."

R.C.'s little sister, Naomi, was my age but I never saw her in town except during the school year, and even then she only came once in a while. She always seemed skittish, kind of like a cat that's been kicked around too many times. I'd liked her from the first time I met her, and Gramma knew it. Gramma used to ask about her, if I'd seen her or how she looked, and when I'd hear her talking to Grampa about Naomi, she always called her a "poor little thing" and would tell Grampa, "It's a crime what's going on out there, Earl. A crime. Since that little girl's mother died, I don't think one nice thing has happened to her, and now's she being mother and daughter in that house."

R.C. was waiting for me on his rickety front porch, and the first thing he noticed was the canvas lunch bag I had slung over my shoulder.

"Whatcha got there, Hiram?"

"Gramma made me a lunch."

"Granny made you a lunch? What a sisbaby! We ain't going camping, we're going fishing, and nobody takes no lunch on a little fishing trip. That big old bag's gonna be in our way all day long." He reached for it. "Let me see what your granny packed."

"These are for Naomi," I said as I pulled out the cookies and handed the bag to R.C. "She around?"

"Naomi!" R.C. yelled. "Hey, Naomi, get yourself out here!" He snatched the cookies out of my hand. "Your *boyfriend* brung you something."

My face turned red. "I'm not her boyfriend, R.C.," I said, even though I wished I was, "Gramma sent those for her." R.C. ignored me and waited for Naomi to open the front door.

When she came out on the porch, she looked mad. "R.C., would you just shush up? Pa's still sleeping." She had her hair in pigtails, as always, and wore the same faded flour-sack dress I'd seen her in at school. "Hey, Hiram." She smiled when she saw me, and I felt my face turn red again.

"Hey, Naomi. My gramma sent something for you." I pointed to the wax paper bundle R.C. held in one hand.

"Sweets from your sweetie," R.C. teased. "Ain't Hiram a regular old Romeo? Your other boyfriends gonna be jealous they find out about this, Naomi."

Naomi walked down the front steps to R.C. and held out her hand. With anybody else, R.C. would've eaten the cookies himself, or crumbled them up, or tossed them on the roof. With Naomi, he handed them to her with a smile.

Naomi unwrapped the cookies. "Gosh, Hiram, your granny sure is nice." She took a big bite of one and said with her mouth full, "Wish I could go fishing with ya'll, but I got chores to do, and then I got to fix lunch for Pa when he wakes up." She wrapped the cookies in the wax paper and trotted up the porch steps. "Tell your granny thanks, Hiram," she said before she went back inside the house. "And good luck fishing. I hope R.C. brings back some fish for supper."

I watched the door close behind her and wished I could have thought of something nice or clever to say to her. Instead, I just stood there like a post until R.C. punched me in the shoulder. "C'mon, Rome-ee-o. We don't got all day for you to stand here gawkin' at my little sister."

We were barely back on the road in front of the Rydells' house before R.C. was rummaging through my lunch bag.

"I told Gramma I didn't need that much lunch, but she made me take it all."

"Biscuits. Mm, still warm." R.C. pulled out two, shoved one into his mouth, and slung the bag over his shoulder. "Let me haul this bundle for you, Hiram. We's walkin' a ways to get to the good fishin' hole, and you're so little, you'd get wore out carryin' this load the whole way." He ate the other biscuit and fished around inside the bag. "Sausage." He pulled out a handful of dark brown sausage links. "This is good stuff, Hiram boy." R.C. ate as we walked, stuffing himself with the loot Gramma had packed. When we were still a ways from our fishing hole, he belched and handed the half-empty bag back to me. "Your granny does know how to cook, Hiram, that's one sure thing. You carry this for a while."

By noon we were both hungry, and we filled up on Gramma's sandwiches, thick slices of homemade bread with a slab of honey ham between them. The bottom of the sack held a dozen gingersnaps, which we finished off after the sandwiches were gone. We saved the two apples to eat on the way home.

Though I loved spending time at the river, I never got any good at fishing. Most of the time, I'd pull up my line to see a bare hook stripped of its bait by a sneaky catfish. R.C. tried to show me how to tell if a fish was nibbling at my bait, but I never caught on. That old cane pole didn't slow R.C. down at all; he seemed to snag fish at will. Every time he hooked one, he'd laugh and jerk it out of the river onto the shore where he'd let it flap and flail on the ground. If it was too small, he'd snap it in the head with his finger to stun it, take it off his hook, and toss it back into the water. "Ain't worth my time, little fish," he'd say, "You eat some more of Hiram's bait and work on growing. Maybe next year I'll come back and catch you for Naomi's frying pan."

The keepers he put on a stringer, a woven cord with a three-inch nail tied to its end, anchored with a rock on the riverside. To add a fish to the stringer, R.C. would work the nail up through the fish's gills and pull it out of its mouth, then hammer the nail back in the ground with a rock and toss the fish into the water to keep them fresh until we went home.

After lunch, R.C. got restless. He had a few keepers and didn't pay much attention to his fishing line after he cast it into the river. I enjoyed sitting there, full of Gramma's lunch, watching the thick green water flow past, hearing the locusts buzz in the brush around us, feeling the hot Mississippi sun on my back. R.C. didn't like silence; he wanted to talk, mostly about things I had no interest in.

"Hiram, ain't them Remington brothers strange? Dancing round in their underwear. Dang, but that is stuh-range."

"Maybe they were too hot."

"Hot! Maybe they's fairies!"

"Huh?"

"Fairies. You know, *queer*. Pa thinks so."

I had no idea what R.C. was talking about, so I shut up and concentrated on my line in the water. Sometimes he could be pretty hard to take.

R.C. turned back to his own pole and for a few minutes was quiet. But only for a few minutes. "Tried me some chewin' tobacca last week. Pa said it'd make me sick, but it didn't. I chawed on that like a man, Pa said. You ever tried it?"

"Naw, my dad would kill me if he heard I'd been trying chew."

"Sheesh, your daddy is the stickenist pa I ever heard of. Seems like you can't do nothin' fun, Hiram, 'cept fish and go out to work on your grandaddy's fields. You're just plain no fun at all."

"I have plenty of fun, R.C., you just don't—"

"Haw, you're the boringest kid I know. Bet you don't even have a girlfriend."

My face turned red. Except for Naomi, I never even talked to girls.

"I got me one: Becca McRay. Last year she liked me to walk her home from school. I seen her underwear, Hiram."

Who cares? I thought. R.C.'s stories were making me tired, and fortunately a tug on his line distracted him for a moment. He jerked a smallish catfish onto the shore; it flopped and glistened in the sun, snapping its head and pointed stingers from side to side.

"Hoo-boy, this one's a little fighter!" R.C. stood out of the fish's way as it thrashed on the ground. When it quit flipping around, he stunned it and held it up.

"Hey, Hiram, watch this." R.C. held the catfish tight in his left hand and had the nail of his fish line in the other. "Whatcha think's in his eyes?" He pressed the nail gently against the fish's eye. The fish jerked when the nail touched it, but R.C. held it firm. Gradually he pressed harder and harder with the nail until it punctured the eye and clear fluid trickled out. "Shoot, no blood." He took less time with its other eye, jabbing it with the nail, then working the point deep into the socket. "Hey, this little old catfish is just like Mr. Paul. 'Look at me, I can't see!'" I felt like I was going to throw up, but I did nothing to stop R.C. He kept poking that fish until it flinched and snapped its stingers into R.C.'s hand. "Ow! Hell dammit, this thing stung me!" He threw the fish to the ground and grabbed his hand. "Ow, ow, ow, that burns." He sucked the wound, then spit. "I hate catfish! Them stingers hurt worse than Pa's belt."

And he wasn't finished.

He picked up the fish line nail, bent over the fish, and jabbed the nail into its side. Blood oozed out. R.C. jabbed it again and again until it was pockmarked with bloody holes. Then he threw the nail down and rested one ragged sneaker on the fish. "Lookit, Hiram, I'm gonna squash its guts out." He stood on one leg, letting his full weight come down on it for a second before he slipped and fell.

I couldn't stand it anymore, so I grabbed a stick and knocked the fish into the water. "Geez, R.C., what's the matter with you? Are you sick or something?"

"What's a matter with *you*? It's only a stupid fish; it don't feel nothing. Dang, Hiram, you are one big sisbaby gettin' all cry-ey over a dumb old fish."

"It's no good hurting a fish, R.C. It didn't do anything wrong."

"Stung me, didn't it?" He held up his hand. "I had to teach it a lesson."

"Fish don't learn lessons. They got no brains, R.C. They're just fish."

R.C. shook his head, looked over at the river, and grinned. "Maybe so, but that dead catfish learned it sure won't sting me no more."

I tried to avoid fishing with R.C. after that, but it was hard to say no to him when he asked. Besides, I liked getting out on the Yazoo, and I wasn't sure what R.C. would do to me if I refused to go fishing with him some time.

I didn't want to end up like that fish.

CHAPTER 3

Silence. One early fall morning a few weeks later, I woke up and the house was deathly quiet. The sun gleamed through my bedroom window; it was still morning, but something wasn't right. I sat up in bed and listened. I could hear the morning birds outside and the sounds of cars crossing the bridge over on Fulton Street, but no sounds from the kitchen. No smell of coffee, bacon, sausage, and biscuits from downstairs. Maybe it's earlier than it seems, I thought. I slid out of bed and padded down the back stairs to the kitchen. No coffee brewed on the stove; everything was exactly as neat and clean as Gramma had left it when I went to bed the night before.

"Gramma?" My voice echoed softly in the kitchen. "Gramma? You here?" I walked through the dining room to the double doors that led to Gramma and Grampa's bedroom. The door was ajar, and I nudged it open further with my head as I peered into their room. No one was there. It hadn't ever looked quite the way I saw it then: The sheets were wrinkled and shoved to the foot of the bed. A closet door stood open, and several drawers of Grampa's dresser stuck out. A chair in the corner had been tipped over. The room felt completely empty.

"Grampa? Gramma?" It felt strange to be in the house alone. I wasn't afraid; it just didn't seem regular. I walked back to the kitchen to get something to eat, when I heard the front door open.

"Hiram? Hiram, boy, you back there?" Grampa came into the kitchen wearing his bib overalls over his pajamas. His hair was rumpled, and he looked exhausted, more tired, more beaten than I'd ever seen him.

He walked in just as I was about to take a bite of the gingersnap I had pulled out of the cookie jar, and I was afraid I was going to catch it from him for eating a cookie first thing in the morning. "Sorry, Grampa, but I couldn't find Gramma and didn't know what to eat . . ."

"Come here, son, come here." He reached his arms out to me, and his eyes welled up with tears. At first I didn't recognize the look on his face. He wasn't mad, that I knew. A tear trickled down his cheek. "Come here, son, please come let me hug you." His voice quivered. He wasn't mad at me; he was sad.

I ran to him and buried my face in the bib of his overalls. He held me tight and said, "Oh, Hiram, son, she's gone. What am I going to do?"

"She'll be back, Grampa," I said as gently as I could. "I bet she just went up to Oxford to see Dad and Mom. We can eat breakfast at the River Café, and then you can take me to school. We'll be okay."

Grampa sat down at the kitchen table and pulled me into his lap. "No, son, Gramma's not coming back, not till the good Lord brings her home to us." His eyes were watery and red. "She's gone to glory, Hiram, gone to glory and left me here alone. Oh, what am I going to do?"

Then it hit me: Gramma was dead.

I wrapped my arms around Grampa's neck and hugged him while we cried together, mourning the loss of a wife and grandmother and friend, wondering how we could possibly survive without her.

Dad and Mom came down to Greenwood as soon as they heard about Gramma. They stayed for the funeral, and those days were the only times I had seen Dad and Grampa together without fighting. Maybe it was out of respect for Gramma, or maybe they just didn't have time. I'd never been around anyone's dying before, and I was surprised at how busy the house got. Neighbors brought in food and flowers. Often they stayed late into the night, eating and talking with Grampa and Dad about Gramma. Mom and some neighbor women stayed busy in the kitchen keeping food coming out into the dining room, washing dishes, and finding space for the plates of sliced ham and roast beef, the bowls of potato salad, the peach pies and chocolate cakes, and the loaves of bread that people brought over.

Ralph and Ronnie Remington even came over to pay their respects. Ronnie wore a black suit coat stretched to button across his wide belly; a limp bow tie hung cockeyed from the collar of his white shirt. Ralph wore a blue tuxedo jacket with navy blue pants, shiny at the knees. He carried a champagne bottle with a wide purple bow tied around its neck. Both men looked about as comfortable as cows in a slaughterhouse. The two of them were speaking quickly to each other, their gaze darting around the room at the neighbors, who avoided or ignored them. Ronnie kept wiping his forehead with a gray handkerchief, while Ralph steered him through the crowded living room toward Grampa and Dad. A group of friends and neighbors stood around my dad and grampa, and when they saw the Remingtons approaching, they closed ranks, blocking them from the circle of mourners. Ronnie looked panicked, mopping his forehead faster and faster while whispering to Ralph. Ralph nodded and listened with a hand on his brother's arm to keep him from bolting. I watched him scan the room, looking for an out, hoping to make contact with at least one person.

I gulped when his eyes met mine, and he immediately smiled and walked toward me, pulling Ronnie along. Ronnie kept his head down, glancing nervously from side to side.

"Young Mr. Hillburn, I presume?" said Ralph. "My brother and I, good friends and neighbors of your dear, dear grandmother, are heartbroken at this recent tragedy. Florence, your grandmother, was a champion, you know, well, of course you know, a friend to all who knew her, a kind, gentle lady. Please know that you have our most mournful condolences." He handed the champagne bottle to me and nudged Ronnie in the ribs.

Ronnie glanced at me before lowering his head again. He was crying. "I promised Ralph I wouldn't cry. I did say it. Yes, I did. 'Ralph,' I said, 'I will not cry. No, I won't. Even though,'" his voice quivered, "'even though Florence Hillburn was our best friend in Greenwood.' Of course Ralph won't cry. He's a rock, a real Gibraltar, though if you ask me, a little emotion is a healthy thing once in a while. Some people are just so hard-hearted, you wonder if they have a heart at all. Not that I mean that Ralph is hard-hearted, no, I would never say that. But of course not your sweet grandmother, no, not her. Florence Hillburn was . . . she was a queen of kindness. Yes, I like how that sounds. It suits her: a queen of kindness." He smiled and wiped a tear from his cheek with the back of his hand.

"Did you know that she often brought us dinner? Leftovers is what she called it, but it was a feast. That woman could cook, but she was full of charity, looked out for Ralph and me, not that we can't look out for each other, for ourselves, of course. We're two grown men perfectly capable of taking care of ourselves, and never once did we look for a handout, no, sir, we never looked for someone's charity. Ralph, you know, isn't much interested in cooking—or eating, for that matter—but I can get into the kitchen and put together a meal when I have to. Why, just last night I was frying some eggs to go with toast. A good meal, you know, fried eggs and toast, and we were about to sit down to eat . . . " His voice grew soft and quivery again. "Well, anyway, Florence Hillburn was, oh, yes, she was . . . a queen of kindness." Tears dripped onto his shoes. I felt sorry for Ronnie—and for me. Seeing him so sad made me miss Gramma more than ever.

Ronnie looked wrung out from talking about Gramma, but Ralph was ready to move. "Ahem, well, yes, young Mr. Hillburn, ah, by the way, what is your name, lad?"

"Hiram."

"Of course, Hiram Hillburn. How could I forget that? Many times I've seen you with your grandparents. Noble family you have here, young Harlan."

"Excuse me, Mr. Remington, but I'm Hiram. Harlan's my dad."

"Yes, of course he is. I've known young Harlan for many years, don't you know." He looked around him. "It's clear that your father and grandfather are going to be occupied for some time with all these dear, dear friends. I'm afraid that I really must get Ronnie back home; this has been so shattering for him, so very difficult. Please extend our most severe and kindest sympathy to your family. I apologize for Ronnie's unseemly outpouring of emotion, but your grandmother's demise has come as a real shock to him, and, of course, to me as well." Ralph cleared his throat. "Now we must return to our own abode and deal with our private grief in whatever ways seem to bring us peace." Ralph nodded at me and steered the crying Ronnie back through the living room and out the front door.

When they left, I realized I'd been crying too.

The graveyard ceremony was just as depressing as everything else had been. Watching Gramma's coffin get lowered into that grave just about broke me in half. I can't recall anything the minister said; I felt like my ears were plugged and I was watching everything through watery eyes. After Gramma had been laid to rest, all the friends and neighbors stuck around to talk with Grampa and Dad, and I just wanted to get out of there, so I told Mom I was going back to the car to wait for everyone. She understood, I think, why I needed to go.

When I turned to leave, I saw Naomi Rydell. Her blonde hair was pulled into tight pigtails, and her face looked shiny and freshly scrubbed.

"Hey, Hiram," she said.

"Hey, Naomi. I didn't know you were here."

"I come a little late, and all those people were so crowded around, I just stayed back a ways." She looked sad. "Don't like funerals."

"Me neither." But I was glad to see her. She didn't make me feel any less sorry for my gramma's death; being around her just made me feel better.

"Last funeral I went to was Ma's. Pa wasn't even there, just me and R.C. It was the hardest thing I ever done, and I didn't want to go, but I went anyway because I loved her and wanted her to know that, without a doubt."

"Funerals don't help a whole lot," I said.

Naomi nodded and bit her lower lip. "I still miss her something awful." She tugged my sleeve. "C'mon, Hiram, I'll show you her grave."

We walked to a quiet corner of the cemetery where there were no headstones. Naomi stopped in front of a grave marked only with a thin metal nameplate. Small piles of old flowers were scattered around it.

"Here she is," Naomi said. "Her body, anyway. I know she's not here, of course. She's up in heaven with the angels, so I don't come here much anymore, but I don't think she minds. When I get real lonely and want to talk to her, you know what I do?" She looked hopeful, like she was going to let me in on a secret.

"No, what?"

"At night, when Pa's sleeping, I walk downtown to the Fulton Street Bridge. It's quiet, you know, and real peaceful. I stand right in the middle and look over the railing and watch the water move by. And I think about my mother. And about"—she lowered her head and her voice shook—"and about how much she loved me." Then Naomi looked up, her eyes red and full of tears, and took my hand. "It's a good place for that, Hiram, and I'll share it with you anytime. You get to missing your gramma—or anybody you love—and you just go there and look into the river and you'll feel better. It can be our place."

I was crying again, and the last person in the world I wanted to see me crying was Naomi. I wiped my tears with the back of my hand. "Thanks," I said. "And sorry. This is hard, you know. I'm really going to miss Gramma."

"I know," she said as gently as someone who really does. "I know."

After Gramma's funeral, Dad had to get back to Ole Miss, but Mom planned to stay in Greenwood a few more days to take care of me and Grampa. Before he left, Dad sat down with me at Gramma's kitchen table.

"You doing okay, son? I've been so busy that I really haven't had a chance to talk with you." Dad seemed uncomfortable, like he knew he had to talk to me but didn't know what to say. "This took us all by surprise, Hiram. I hope you understand that only Gramma's body is dead. Her spirit still lives, and we'll be with her again one day." He cleared his throat and said, "Now, your mother wants you to come back to Oxford with her when she leaves next weekend."

"But who'll take care of Grampa? He'll be in this big old house all by himself. He'll be so lonely." My eyes got teary when I thought about Gramma dead in her grave and Grampa sad and all alone. I swallowed hard to keep from sobbing.

"Grampa can take care of himself, Hiram. He's only fifty-five, and he's got lots of friends here in Greenwood."

"Daddy, why don't you and Mom come down here and live again? We can all stay together and help Grampa get along with things. I bet Gramma would like that."

"It's not that easy, son." Dad rubbed the back of his neck and sighed. "I can't see how we could come down here, not now, anyway. I'm in the middle of a semester, and Mom's got that job at Oxford Elementary."

"When school's over, then can we? I like living here with Grampa."

Dad frowned. "Hiram, when we let you come down here to live with Gramma and Grampa, it was never intended to be permanent. We're our own family, and as soon as I'm finished with school, we'll live together again. In a house of our own."

"But this house is big enough for all of us. Why can't we live here?" As far as I was concerned, this was *my* house too. It scared me to think of living anywhere else.

"Because of your grampa. He's been quiet during these funeral days, but pretty soon he'd start in on me again. And frankly, I don't want to live in Greenwood or in Mississippi. I've already started looking for college teaching jobs in the West: Utah, Idaho, Arizona, California. I love the Delta, but there are some things you can't understand that keep it from being a good place for us right now."

"It's good enough for me, Daddy. I like Greenwood. I like this old house."

"Son, you don't know some of the uglier things about the South. I want you to grow up understanding that all men are free and deserve to be treated that way. Ever since I got home from the war, your mother and I have been planning to move west. It'll be good for us, you'll see."

I didn't see. I couldn't. I loved my life in Greenwood. Grampa had warned me about Dad's crazy ideas and that someday he might want to leave Mississippi, but I never believed him.

"What's wrong with Mississippi?"

"You're too young to understand now, but someday you will. I'm just doing what's best for our family."

I knew there was no talking Dad out of it, but I couldn't give up without trying.

"But can I stay here with Grampa?"

"Of course not." Dad's face flushed. "You're my son, and you'll do what I say."

"No, I mean can I still live with Grampa while you're at Ole Miss? I've got a bed here, and I can help him with things, and Mom can still come down on weekends and for the summer vacation. Grampa will be so lonely, Daddy. He'll need me. It'll only be for a little while."

Dad shook his head tiredly and said, "I'll speak to your mother about it, but don't get your hopes up."

But after Dad left for Oxford, Mom told me they decided I could stay if I wanted to.

So I stayed with Grampa in Greenwood. He moped around for a while, but gradually things got back to normal. Ruthanne, a tall, thin Negro woman Grampa hired to cook and clean, knew how to cook everything Gramma ever had, and some other things as well. She worked five and a half days a week—she had Sundays off and didn't come in until Monday afternoons—kept the house immaculate, and kept me and Grampa stuffed with delicious food. But Grampa would no longer eat in the kitchen. "Just doesn't feel right," he told me one night while we sat on the front porch swing watching for meteors. "That old kitchen feels wrong without Florence in it. You can eat there if you want, Hiram, but I'm going to have to eat in the dining room from now on. There's too much Florence in that kitchen, and I can't stand to eat in there without her around."

Sometimes at night, late, when it seemed like the house was covered with a heavy damp blanket of darkness, I would hear Grampa moving around downstairs. Sounds in the kitchen. Then muffled movement in the living room. Once in a while I'd hear the front door open and close. It made my chest ache to think of my grandpa down there, lost and looking for his wife, searching their familiar places for memories of her.

That turned out to be my last year in Greenwood. When school was out in Oxford, Mom came down to live with me and Grampa, and Dad announced that he was almost done with graduate school. He figured he'd finish everything up by the middle of July, right after my ninth birthday. He'd already started hearing back from some colleges about jobs, and at the end of June he called us from Ole Miss to say that he'd received a letter and contract from Arizona State College, and we'd be moving to Tempe in August, just in time for the new school year. "It's going to be a new life," he said. "A whole new life."

A life without Grampa, a life away from my home. I knew I'd hate it, and I hated my dad for all his plans to rip me out of Greenwood and ruin my life. Right then I swore that I'd never be happy in Arizona.

That night, mad and sad, I went to the Fulton Street Bridge for the first time since Gramma died. I stood in the spot Naomi had described and watched the dark water of the Yazoo swirl under the bridge. I thought about Gramma and Grampa and how much I'd miss them when we left Mississippi. I prayed to be able to stay. I begged God to stop Dad from dragging me to Arizona.

And I prayed that Naomi would show up at the bridge that night so I could explain why we were leaving, so I could say good-bye. More than anyone, she would understand how I felt.

I stayed on the bridge as late as I dared. Naomi never came, and before I left, I looked down into the Yazoo one last time and whispered, "Gramma, Grampa, Naomi, I'll come back. I promise."

CHAPTER 4

The last time Grampa and Dad talked to each other was when Dad announced he was moving us to Arizona.

Grampa blew his stack. "Arizona! Why in hell would you want to live in that desert? That's my only grandchild you got there, Harlan. How can you take him away from his home, from his grampa?" They argued for a while, Grampa swearing and shouting, Dad yelling right back. As usual, the only thing their arguing did was make them both madder.

On the morning that we left, Grampa refused to help us load up the car; he just stood on the front porch and watched. When it was time to leave, Dad slid behind the wheel and said, "Say good-bye to your grampa, Hiram. No telling when you'll see him again." Mom glared at Dad a moment and then sighed and walked over to hug Grampa.

She whispered something in his ear that made him smile and pat her on the back. "Thanks, Earl," she said as she walked back to the car. "Thanks for everything, especially for taking good care of Hiram."

Then it was my turn to say good-bye, and I didn't want to. "Come here, boy," Grampa said as he opened his arms to welcome me. I ran to him and wrapped my arms around his wide body, burying my face in the bib of his blue overalls. I felt him tremble. "I'm going to miss you, son," he said with a catch in his voice. "You be a good boy in Arizona, and make sure you don't go forgetting your grampa."

"I won't, Grampa." I struggled not to cry. "I promise." I gave him one last hug and ran back to the car.

"Harlan, Dee," Grampa called to my parents, "ya'll know that boy is welcome here anytime. I'd be awful glad to have him spend summers with me, and I'd treat him right." Mom nodded and waved as Dad drove us away from the house without even looking back. Grampa stood on the porch and waved until we turned the corner onto Cotton Street.

We survived our first Arizona summer and settled into Tempe quickly. Dad started work at Arizona State College, and Mom stayed home and started having babies. It always seemed ironic to me that once we left the Delta in fertile Mississippi for the barren Arizona desert, Mom and Dad suddenly started producing kids at the rate of one per year for four years: Joseph was born about a year after we got to Tempe, 1949; then came Emma, Eliza, and finally Brigham in 1952. Arizona turned out to be everything Dad had hoped it would be. He seemed happier than ever, and I wasn't sure if it was because of his job at the college, our new lives in Arizona, or just being away from Mississippi.

It took me a year to get over leaving Grampa and Greenwood, and even though I eventually adjusted to living in Tempe, the annual invitation from Grampa to spend the summer in Greenwood would get me mad all over again. When I turned into a teenager, I got older and bolder, and I'd argue with Dad about it, but he was stubborn as a stump.

"This is your home now, Hiram. Your family's here, and you're staying here. If Grampa really wants to see you, he'll come out here and visit on my terms. I will not have you spending three months in Mississippi getting a head full of your grampa's Southern nonsense."

"But he's my grampa."

"That's enough, Hiram Hillburn. You say one more word on this, and you'll be mighty sorry!" Dad's eyes got wide and mean-looking, and his face turned red just like it used to when he argued with Grampa, and even though I was older and bolder, I knew there'd only be trouble if I pushed him any more.

Except for the regular fights with Dad, the last few years went smooth enough. I grew a few inches, did pretty well in school, and learned how to avoid Dad. Those years, our worst battles always started over my wanting to visit Grampa and Mississippi. The last time we fought about it, I used every excuse I could think of. Finally, I said, "He's your dad, my grampa. It's family, even if you don't like it. You ought to want to go back as bad as I do."

"I don't need you to be telling me what I should and should not do. There are some things, Hiram, you just can't understand. Maybe when you're older, you will."

"But Grampa invited me. You've *got* to let me go."

"You listen to me: I will not have one of my children giving me orders, understand? Don't you be bothering me about this again." He glared at me with that mean look I'd seen him use with Grampa. "And I mean it!"

I wanted to bother Dad about it, I wanted to bother him bad. *He* should be the one trying to get to Greenwood; *he* should be the one most concerned about Grampa. It made me furious that he didn't care at all about his own father or about what I wanted.

I was almost sixteen in April 1955, when Grampa's annual invitation to Greenwood arrived, but this letter was different. He'd had a small stroke. Not a serious one, he said, but he'd need someone to help him for a while until he got his strength back. "The stroke and the diabetes Doc Peterson says I've got have slowed me down some," he wrote. "There's plenty of work that needs doing, son, and until I get feeling good again, I don't know how much I'll be able to do by myself."

He'd also written to Mom, and whatever he said must have convinced her, because she took it up with Dad as soon as he got home from work. Before he even set his briefcase down by the door, she started on him. "Earl is going to need some more help, Harlan; Ruthanne's already got her hands full."

"You know I don't like the idea of Hiram being in Greenwood," Dad said.

"It's his being with your father that you don't like. Your dad is not going to poison him one bit and you know it. Hiram's nearly sixteen, and you know better than anyone that he's got his own mind. It'll be good for him to spend some time with his grandfather, and it will do wonders for Earl."

"I don't like it, Dee, not one bit."

"How can you not like it? He's your *father*, Hiram's grandfather. And we owe it to him. If he hadn't been willing to tend Hiram those years we were in Oxford, I don't know what we would've done. You wouldn't have finished Ole Miss, that's for sure. Besides, maybe doing service for someone else all summer will be good for Hiram."

Dad said nothing. Mom had him backed into a corner.

"Harlan, let the boy go. Help your father. Maybe it'll soften his heart. . . . Maybe it'll soften yours too."

Dad sighed. "All right, but not until school's out, not for the entire summer, and he's got to be back before school starts again."

I couldn't believe Mom had won.

I couldn't believe Dad had given in.

I smiled, not because Dad had lost, but because I was actually going to Greenwood. Dad noticed my grin, and when

Mom left the room, he said, "You think you won something big, don't you? Well, you're going to find out that I know some things you don't. Greenwood's not going to be what you expect, Hiram. You're older now, you'll see. And I'm sorry for what you'll see."

I had no idea what he was talking about, and I didn't care. All I knew was that finally I was going back to Greenwood . . . and to Grampa.

Dad stalled my trip as long as he could. When school was out in June, he said we couldn't afford the train fare to Mississippi. It wasn't until the middle of July that he announced that we had enough money for me to go. He'd already booked a ticket on the Santa Fe Rail Line and told me I'd be leaving August nineteenth.

When the nineteenth arrived, Mom took me to the train station in Phoenix. It was no surprise that Dad wasn't there. He said he had some meetings on campus, but I was sure that he just didn't care enough about me to come. That didn't bother me, because I felt the same way about him. I was looking forward to seeing Grampa again, but more than anything, I was glad to be away from Dad for a while.

"Your grandfather said Ruthanne will meet you at the station in Greenwood," said Mom. "Behave yourself on the train, and be sure to pay attention to the stops. I know you'll be good to Grampa, Hiram, but you make sure you look after him the best you can. And mind him and Ruthanne while you're in that house." Then she quickly hugged me. The train's steam whistle sounded and the porters called all aboard. "I love you, son," she said as I stepped up into the passenger car. "Have a wonderful time with Grampa."

After I stowed my bags and found my seat, I felt excited and sad at the same time; I would miss Mom and the kids, but I couldn't wait to get back home to Grampa and Mississippi.

CHAPTER 5

I was surprised by how little I remembered of Mississippi. I'd forgotten the heat, the heavy humidity that made me sweat all the time. The deep green bushes and trees everywhere seemed foreign, and it was strange to look out the train window and not see mountains anywhere. When our train finally pulled into Greenwood, I started worrying. What had I done, I wondered, leaving Arizona for a place I hardly remembered?

I collected my bags and stood on the platform of the Greenwood station. A few cars lined the redbrick street in front of the station, and across the street I recognized one building at least, the Crystal Grill, one of Grampa's favorite restaurants. I sat down on a bench to wait for Ruthanne and to try to make some sense of this town my dad and I had grown up in. Most women on the sidewalks wore dresses and large hats. Many of the men wore baggy short-sleeved white shirts, a few had on ties. It was early afternoon, and people seemed in a hurry to get somewhere—probably to find a place to escape the heat. I could hear snatches of conversation in the same heavy Mississippi accent that Mom and Dad sometimes lapsed into when they talked to each other at home, and it seemed like the most natural kind of speech in the world. I couldn't figure out why Dad hated it here; it seemed like the homiest place on earth to me, and the longer I stood there, the happier I was to be away from Dad and back where I belonged.

Another big difference between Greenwood and Tempe was the Negroes. There had been a few Negro porters on the train, but I was surprised by how many I saw around the Greenwood station. The freight workers on the platform were all Negroes, of course, but so were almost half the people around the station. The Negro women wore simple cotton farm dresses without hats; most of the Negro men and boys wore blue bib overalls, the same kind Grampa always wore.

"Hiram. Hiram Hillburn, is that you?" It was Ruthanne, and I turned to greet her. She smiled, reached out, and held me by my shoulders. "Child, have you grown! Arizona surely has been good to you." I was nearly six feet tall; when I was a boy, Ruthanne used to tower over me, but now I was able to look her in the eye. "You're just like Mr. Harlan; if you weren't so fresh-looking, I'd swear you were Mr. Hillburn's own boy, not his grandchild."

That was the last thing I wanted to hear. "I'm nothing like my dad, Ruthanne. Nothing at all."

"Shucks, you're your daddy's son whether you like it or not, Mr. Hiram, but I guess at your age, you'd just as soon not admit it." She pointed to my bags. "Let's get those down into the truck and get you home. Your grampa can't wait to see you."

When I tried to pick them up, she stopped me. "You been riding that train for three days. Let Bobo over here carry them; he's got nothing to do right now." She nodded to a Negro boy who looked about my age standing near the edge of the platform. "Bobo," she called, "come on over here and carry Mr. Hiram's bags down to the truck."

He gave her a bored look and didn't move.

"Get yourself over here this minute," she snapped, "and don't you be giving me any of that sass."

Bobo sauntered over. His clothes set him apart from the other Negroes I had seen around the station. Wearing black leather dress shoes, pants, and white shirt, he looked nothing like a country boy from the Delta. He smirked at me as he stood next to Ruthanne.

"Mr. Hiram," Ruthanne said, "this here is Bobo Till, my cousin's nephew; he just come down from Chicago and's been waiting on his train up to Money."

"Hi, Bobo," I said.

He only nodded in return, and Ruthanne didn't like it. "Don't you get on so rude," she said as she nudged him in the side with her arm, "you talk when you been talked to."

Bobo rolled his eyes and then stuttered, "H-hi, H-Hi-ram."

"That's better," said Ruthanne. "Now, you pick up Mr. Hiram's things and help me get them down to the truck. And hurry up, or you're liable to miss your train."

"I b-b-been on the train all the way from Chicago, Ruthanne. I'm too tired to be carrying somebody else's old b-bags."

"That's okay, Ruthanne," I said, "I can handle my own things. Just got this duffel and the one suitcase. They're not heavy at all."

"See," Bobo said with a smirk. "No need for me to be carrying his b-bags. B-besides, it's too hot down here for me to be hauling stuff all over."

Ruthanne turned on him with her hands on her hips. "Emmett Till, you do what you're told to do, when you're told to do it. You've been raised better than that, and I know it." She glared at him until he went over and picked up my duffel bag. Satisfied that he had done at least part of what she had asked, Ruthanne turned and headed down the stairs off the platform and into the street.

"Ain't b-been raised to be nobody's old p-porter," he muttered so Ruthanne couldn't hear. Then he looked at me and said, "Don't see nobody carrying my b-bags around for me," and followed Ruthanne.

I picked up my suitcase and walked alongside Bobo. "So you're from Chicago, huh? You a Cubs fan?"

"Naw." Bobo shrugged. "It's dang hard to be a Cubs fan

these days. What are they, twenty-something games behind B-Brooklyn? Unless they have a decent chance at the p-pennant, I've decided b-being a Cubs fan is a waste of time. B-b-besides, I got b-better things to do back home than worry about b-baseball. Hey, do me a favor," he said as he paused at the top of the stairs, "and hold this for a second." He handed me my duffel bag. I took it and he went down the stairs without me. I stood there feeling dumb as a brick.

Bobo stayed a few steps ahead of me as we walked down the street to Grampa's blue Ford pickup. Ruthanne had just dropped the tailgate when we arrived, and right before she turned around to see us, Bobo took my duffel bag from me and winked. "Thanks," he said before he handed it to Ruthanne to put into the bed of the truck. He turned and headed back to the train platform without saying good-bye.

As we pulled away from the station, we drove past a blonde-haired girl about my age. She walked with her head down like she was trying to be invisible. "Who's that girl?" I asked Ruthanne.

"Naomi Rydell." Ruthanne shook her head and sighed. "Too bad about that little girl; the things she's been through make a body wonder if God's in heaven."

"R.C.'s sister? I would've never recognized her." Seeing Naomi, even for a moment, stirred a warm spot in my chest and made me remember that there was more than just Grampa that I cared about in Greenwood. "But what things are you talking about?"

"Same old, same old. Her no-account brother is in one

scrape after another, and if that wasn't enough, her low-down father treats her worse than a family mule. Sleeps all day, drinks all night, and never does a lick of work. Poor girl's running that house, trying to keep that pitiful family together the best she can. Lord knows it can't be nothing but misery in that shack out there on River Road."

Would Naomi remember me?

I sure hoped she would.

When I stepped through the front door of Grampa's house, I closed my eyes and took a deep breath through my nose, and memories came flooding back. Gramma working in the kitchen. Grampa sitting in his chair smoking a cigar and reading the paper. Waking up mornings in my dad's old room to the smell of coffee and sausage. This was it. I was back.

Ruthanne had gone ahead of me into the living room. "He's here, Mr. Hillburn," she said. "The boy's come home."

The rustle of newspapers and then Grampa's voice. "Hiram? Hiram, son, come in here and let me look at you!"

When I entered the living room, Grampa was in his favorite chair. On one side of it stood a wheelchair with a pair of wooden crutches lying across the arm rests. Grampa beamed when he saw me.

"Hey, Grampa."

"Don't 'Hey, Grampa' me. Come here and give me a hug."

I went to his chair and bent over to hug him. His cheeks were rough with stubble and paler than I remembered, but his arms felt as solid and strong as ever. "Welcome back, welcome back, son," he said softly as he held me. "It's so good to have you home again."

When he let go, he wiped his eyes with his finger and smiled. "You've turned into a young man, Hiram. Not much like that little boy who used to run around here and steal Gramma's gingersnaps."

I didn't know what to say. It was hard not to stare at the wheelchair; Grampa didn't seem right, didn't seem like I remembered—or at least like I wanted him to be.

"Don't worry about these old doodads," he said, pointing to the wheelchair and crutches. "They were just temporary help till I got my blood circulating right and my legs working again. I'd be lying if I said that stroke hadn't hit me hard at first, but now I'm getting around pretty good for an old man; a little slow and stiff sometimes, but I get around when I have to.

"Sit down." He waved his hand at me. "You've had a long train ride and must be worn out." He raised up in his chair and called to the kitchen, "Ruthanne, this boy needs some cold lemonade, and see if you can round up a plate of some of those cookies I've been smelling these past two days."

In a moment Ruthanne returned and set a glass of lemonade and a plate of gingersnaps on the table beside me and handed Grampa a tall glass of iced tea. He took a drink and squinted as if he were in pain. "Dammitall, Ruthanne, this tastes like brown water. Can't I get something to sweeten it up?"

"Now, Mr. Hillburn"—Ruthanne shook her head—"you know what Doc Peterson says about you and sugar. I'm just doing what he asked me to do."

"Damn diabetes," Grampa muttered as he handed the glass back to her. "I'm not thirsty anyway. Guess I'll just enjoy getting reacquainted with my oldest grandson for a while."

As soon as Ruthanne left the room, Grampa said, "Hiram, hand me a couple of those gingersnaps, will you? What Ruthanne and Doc Peterson don't know won't hurt them any."

Grampa nibbled on the cookies while I told him about Joseph, Emma, Eliza, and Brigham. He was full of questions about them, and often pulled out an envelope that held snapshots Mom had sent him over the years to look at while I talked about my brothers and sisters. "We've got to get them to come out here for a visit sometime," he said. "I need to see the rest of my grandchildren, and they need to see me and Gramma's house."

We talked for a couple more hours, but Grampa never once asked about Dad.

And I didn't offer to talk about him. Being around Grampa again made me feel good, and reminded me why I hated Dad for making us move to Arizona. I didn't care what Ruthanne or anybody said: I wasn't like my father. I was my grampa's boy, always had been, always would be.

The next morning, I felt kind of strange when I woke up in my old bed in Dad's room and smelled the familiar breakfast aromas coming up from the kitchen. For a moment I felt like I was a little kid again and Gramma was down in the kitchen cooking breakfast. The moment soon passed, but I lay in bed for a long time savoring the warm feelings and memories that washed over me in my favorite place in the world. Ruthanne finally had to call me down for breakfast.

It was good to be back in Greenwood. I had come back home, and I was free.

CHAPTER 6

Grampa didn't get up for breakfast. "Your granddaddy doesn't sleep well these days, and some nights he's up late at those Council meetings," Ruthanne explained, "so you just as well go ahead and eat, Mr. Hiram. He said that if you want, after breakfast you can borrow his truck—if it's not already borrowed; you ask me, he's too free and easy lending that truck around—and take a look around town. He'll be ready for you by lunchtime, so plan on being back by then."

After breakfast I went out into the backyard to look around; things hadn't changed much. Around the side of the house and through the bushes between our yards, I could see Ralph's and Ronnie's paths still clearly worn in the Remingtons' yard. Ralph Remington had just come out the back door and started on his path when he saw me. At first he looked spooked.

"Harlan? Harlan Hillburn, is that you?" He squinted to get a better look at me.

"Nosir, it's me, Hiram; I'm Harlan's son." It made me a little mad to be confused for my father, but I knew Ralph was an egg or two short of a dozen.

Still squinting, he took a few steps and stopped when he was as close to me as his path allowed. "Harlan's married? And you're his boy?" He looked me up and down. "Spitting image of your father, son, pure-D spitting image. I'd a sworn you were Harlan himself, yes, sir. A plain mirror image of your father. Not your father now, no, not that, but your father when he was your age. How old are you anyway, son?"

"Sixteen."

"Sixteen. Ah, a fine age to be, sixteen. I remember when I myself was sixteen, some, let's see, well, too many years ago. Sixteen is half of thirty-two, you know, and I can still recall being thirty-two. Not a bad year, what I can remember of it, not bad at all. No, at thirty-two a man is at the brink of middle age, still young enough to enjoy life, but old enough to know what's worth enjoying. Yes, yes, young Hiram, thirty-two is a *fine* age." He paused and looked carefully at me again. "But you don't look thirty-two at all, I don't care what you say."

"I didn't say I was—"

"And I can't for the life of me imagine why a lad your age would want to go around making folks think he's older than he really is. You've got to take pride in who and what you are, Hiram. Pride. The nation's founded on it, and if you can't take pride in yourself, if you insist on hiding behind falsehoods, well, you're headed for trouble with a capital T. Besides, boy, anyone with a noodle of sense would know with a single look that you're not even close to thirty-two years old. Hogwash! It's complete foolishness for you to even *dream* you could pass for a man of that mature age. I tell you, no, let me guess." He pointed at my chest. "I daresay you're not much older than sixteen. There, yes. Sixteen."

He waited for me to say something, but I had no idea what to say.

"Well, tell me, boy, am I right? Are you sixteen or not?"

"Yessir."

He jerked his arm back and snapped his fingers. "I knew it! Just plain knew it. Thirty-two, what on earth could you have been thinking? Trying to pull the wool over my eyes, weren't you? I hardly ever get an age wrong, no, not when you know as many people as I know for as long as I've known them. So, Harlan, what are you up to today?"

"Hiram, sir. Harlan's my father."

"Yes, yes, I knew that. So, Hiram, what are you up to today?"

"I'm thinking about going fishing if I can find some gear in Grampa's garage."

"Fishing? Fishing, now there's a messy game. And a capital waste of time, if you ask me. Of course, it can be made better if accompanied by the right spirits, as in libations. A few good drinks can make any fishing trip worthwhile, but by and large it's a national waste of time, if you ask me, a waster of men's hours and nature's fruits. Sit around all day with a line in the water hoping to catch one of God's silver creatures of the water world. And when you do catch one, well, you treat it in the most inhumane manner, slicing it from tail to throat, sliding your thumb along its spine to dump its guts. Ugh." He shivered. "The entire process is far too messy, if you ask me. A wise man finds a cool place to sit, a place where he can knock back a few cold drinks and worry about the other more foolish of his kind who are out in the hot sun hoping to lure a catfish to their bait. Fishing. Oh, yes, you're thinking of fishing. Well, Harlan, does your father know you're planning on going out to the river alone? Can be dangerous, oh, mighty dangerous."

I felt like I was trapped in quicksand; would he ever get anything right? Would he ever stop talking? I took a deep breath and said, "Nosir, my father's back in—"

"Going behind your father's back, are you? Well, your little deception here with me would suggest you might tend to that sort of game. But I tell you, Harlan—"

"Hiram. I'm Hiram."

"What's that?"

"I'm Hiram. My father's Harlan."

"I knew that. Of course I knew that. But as I was saying, Harlan, you best let your father know you're going fishing. No telling what kind of trouble you might get into out there on the water. Why, just last year we had a boy drown over in Tallahatchie County. Fishing alone. No one knows for sure how he ended up in the water, but he was good and dead anyway. You stay out of that water if you know what's good for you, son." Ralph's eyes started wandering, like he was losing focus. Or maybe he was hearing voices. He looked down the path toward the street, then behind him to his back door. A moment later his gaze came back on me.

"Harlan? Harlan Hillburn, is that you?" He squinted at me again.

"Yessir, Mr. Ralph. And it's good to see you." I waved and headed for the safety of the garage. "You have yourself a good day, and please say hello to Mr. Ronnie for me."

When I was out of sight, I watched him. Still on the path, he looked confused, and then worried. Finally, he looked around, shook his head, and said, "Funny, I could have sworn I saw Harlan Hillburn today." Then he started up the path to the sidewalk and headed downtown.

That was my first conversation with Ralph Remington since I was a kid, and if I could help it, it would be my last. I'd never known anyone who could talk in such circles. When I was little, Gramma and Grampa had always told me to stay away from the Remington brothers, and now I knew why. Ralph's circular talking would make a kid want to swear off talking to adults for the rest of his life.

I couldn't remember exactly where Grampa kept his fishing stuff, so I rummaged around the garage until I found a fishing pole and some tackle. I put the gear in the back of Grampa's truck and headed north out of town. Though it was still morning, the Delta air was already hot and thick, and the breeze that blew through my open window did more to make me sweaty than it did to cool me off.

I took Old Money Road through the tiny cotton gin community somebody with a weird sense of humor had named Money and headed for a spot on the Tallahatchie River where Grampa and I used to fish. It felt good to be in the Delta again, out among the green cotton fields. The air smelled rich with dampness and earth, and whenever the engine slowed, I could hear the steady drone of locusts everywhere.

After I'd driven a few miles north of Money, I realized that one cotton field looks pretty much like another, that farm roads all look alike, and that back when I was fishing with Grampa, I hadn't been paying attention to where we were going.

But it didn't really matter, because I just wanted to get out on the river, not to fish but because I had always loved the solitude of sitting on the banks, enjoying the lazy movement of water and the beauty of the Delta. Not far past a few tar-paper shanties where Negro field hands lived, I caught a glimpse of the river, so I turned down the next road and followed it through the brush to a small clearing on the banks of the Tallahatchie.

In five minutes I was settled against the base of a tree on the riverbank watching my line tugging against the current. The thick green water seemed hypnotic or soothing or something, and the anger I'd had for Dad, the worries about Grampa, and any other cares I'd brought with me to Mississippi were swept away, and for the first time in a long time, maybe the first time since I'd left Greenwood, I felt content. The sights, the sounds, the smells, everything around me was familiar, and I was home. All that peaceful stuff, though, made me sleepy. I closed my eyes and dozed for several minutes until a sound I thought I had dreamed woke me up.

Splashing. Thrashing in water. And someone calling for help.

I set my pole down and stood up. "Help!" cried a panicked voice from downstream. "Somebody help me!" I jogged along the banks toward the sound. "Help, hey, somebody!" The voice was garbled, choking. At the next clearing I saw someone almost in the middle of the river, flailing in the water. He was too far out for me to reach with a branch or stick.

"Hey, hey you!" I yelled. "Hang on. I'm coming in." I kicked off my shoes and dove into the Tallahatchie. It took five or six strokes to reach him, and as soon as I got close, he crashed both arms into my head and thrashed around so wildly that I couldn't grab him; finally he did exactly what our lifesaving merit badge instructor had said drowning victims always do: He threw his arms around my neck and clamped on like a two-ton crawdad. We sank in a hurry, and his grip tightened, choking me, as soon as the water closed over our heads.

That's when *I* panicked. I knew we'd both be dead if I didn't do something, so with my free arm I reached back as far as I could and punched him in the face. That only loosened his grip, so I jammed my knee up into his crotch. A burst of air bubbles blew out of his mouth and his grip slackened enough for me to shove him away, scissors-kick back to the surface, and take deep gulps of air. He floated up a moment later, taking what looked like his last breath. I swam around behind him, popped him in the head again to make sure he was going to cooperate, looped my arm under his chin, and side-kicked us to shore. He floated along without a struggle.

It was a Negro boy, and his short dark hair glistened and dripped water as I dragged him up on the riverbank. He moaned and twisted over on his stomach once I had him on land, so I stood away and let him figure out where he was before I said anything. Other than the rise and fall of his back, he didn't move for several seconds, then he got up on his hands and knees and puked river water.

"You'll feel better soon," I said. "It's good when your body gets all that stuff out."

The boy shook his head, coughed, then vomited again. He stayed on all fours for a minute, then turned over and sat on the grass, resting his arms on his knees and letting his head hang like he was exhausted. He looked familiar; his clothes were different, but I recognized him. "Bobo? We met at the train station; you were with Ruthanne."

"Call me Emmett. Family calls me B-Bobo, but I'm trying to get rid of that nickname." He peeled off his T-shirt and wrung out the water.

"Good thing I caught you when I did," I said, "or you'd've been fish bait."

"You hit me." He pressed the back of his wrist against his

bleeding lip and then held his arm out and showed me the blood on his wrist.

"You would've drowned both of us, so I figured I had only one chance to make sure you'd let go. You going to be okay?"

"Long as you d-d-don't tell anybody."

"You get in trouble if your parents find out?"

He shook his head and held out his hands for me to pull him up. "Got my reputation to maintain," he said as he stood up. "I d-d-don't want my old country cousins having a good laugh on me. When my uncle heard I couldn't swim, he told me to stay away from the river, but I figured a little old river's not going to hurt me. Anyway, I'd appreciate it if you don't say nothing to nobody."

"Sure, but I gotta know, how come you were in the river if you don't know how to swim?"

"I spent all night in my uncle's shack out this way and was b-bored stiff. For a good time around here, my cousins think hanging out at B-Bryant's store is as good as it gets. Hey, I'm from Chicago, and we got lots more action up there. I figured if I was going to be here for a couple weeks, I'd b-better take a look around and see if there was anything I could do that would be a little more interesting than chopping cotton or playing checkers at B-Bryant's Meat and Grocery. This morning I followed an old p-path from my uncle's shack and it came to this river, and 'cause I had nothing b-better to do, I stood around chucking rocks in the water."

"Chucking rocks usually don't get you into the river," I said.

Emmett stood up. "Yeah, well, when I was p-picking up rocks along the shore to chuck, one b-bit me." He held up his middle finger that had a chunk of missing skin. "Some kind of spiny-backed turtle."

"Snapper. They call them snapping turtles down here."

"Okay, so that old snapper snapped me good, and I thought maybe I'd go after him and b-bring him b-back to my uncle's place. He'd be a good trick to play on somebody's b-bed." Emmett smiled. "I saw him move away from the shore, so I took off my shoes and waded in after him. He kept moving, I kept moving, then I slipped and the old river started p-pushing me downstream. It was a heck of a lot d-deeper than I thought."

He took a shaky breath. "For a while I figured I was never going to see Chicago again. Dang glad you heard me."

"No problem. I was just fishing downstream a ways. Actually, I was napping with my fishing pole and you woke me up."

"Not the first time I've been somebody's b-bad dream. Anyway, now I know what a fish feels like. I think I like Chicago better."

"Maybe you ought to stay away from the Tallahatchie while you're down here. Next time I might not be around to pull you out."

"Don't worry 'b-bout that. I'll be finding me b-better things to do than hang around some old river filled with snapping turtles and sleepy white fishermen." He grinned.

"I gotta find my shoes and head b-back to my uncle's place. It's about lunchtime, and my aunt'll have conniptions if I'm not there to eat."

We walked upstream together until he found his shoes. He sat down and pulled them on, then stood and put on his T-shirt. "I'll see you around," he said as he headed up the path. "Hope the lifeguarding business keeps up for you."

When I got back to my fishing spot, I picked up my pole and reeled in my line. The hook was empty, of course.

I laid the pole on the grass and sat back down under the shade of a cypress tree hoping to go back to sleep, but I still had too much adrenaline pumping through me to relax. When I'd earned that lifesaving merit badge a couple years earlier, I never figured on using it; there's not a whole lot of water in Tempe, and what little there is, is usually in a cement rectangle supervised by a lifeguard. The rescue I'd just done scared me. I could've drowned; Emmett and I both could have ended up dead in the Tallahatchie River. I wondered if anyone would have ever found us. I wondered if Dad would have even cared.

The peace I'd enjoyed earlier was gone, so I picked up my pole, walked back to the truck, and headed home. Grampa would likely be up and ready for lunch by now. I remembered how he felt about Negroes, and didn't plan on saying anything to him about Emmett and the river.

My clothes were still damp when I got home, and when Grampa asked how I got all wet, I lied and told him I'd had a snag on my line pretty far out in the river, and when I went out to try to work it free, I fell in.

"I taught you better than that, Hiram. Any good fisherman can loose a snag if he uses his head. If nothing else, you can just cut the dang line."

I shrugged. "I didn't want to lose my hook and sinker."

"How many times you been fishing since you left Greenwood?" Grampa asked, though he already knew the answer. Dad hated fishing. "If your father ever bothered to take you fishing, you wouldn't have forgotten everything I taught you." He scowled and paused a moment. "No matter. Run upstairs and get changed. You're driving us to the River Café for lunch. Hurry on up, son, 'cause I'm plenty hungry."

After I changed my clothes, I helped him outside and into the truck and climbed behind the wheel. I started the truck and backed down the driveway. "So what have you been doing since they let you out of the hospital?"

"Reading, mostly. Some exercises, learning how to get around, getting the old legs to do what I tell them. And eating Ruthanne's good cooking—more of it than I should. And some folks come around, and we talk about the Councils and what we can do to keep our schools around here right."

I turned onto River Road and headed downtown. "What's wrong with the schools?"

"What's wrong? Hasn't your daddy told you about the desegregation ruling by that rabble-rousing Supreme Court? Bet he's been happier than a pig in mud about all that craziness. I tell you, son, mixing Negroes with our white students is going to ruin our schools and all America, but down here, we're not going to allow it. Some good folks formed White Citizens' Councils to keep things sensible in the Delta. Those damn Yankees think they can tell us how to run our lives, well, they better think again." He looked real serious. "I tell you, son, around here, we're not going to take this integration craziness lying down. Not us, not here, not ever."

The more he talked about the Supreme Court's ruling, the more agitated Grampa became, and I was glad when we pulled up in front of the River Café. Maybe we'd run into enough of his old buddies that he'd have something else to talk about besides schools and Negroes.

I'd had enough tension for one day.

CHAPTER 7

Monday afternoon I convinced Grampa to drive out with me to look at the fields. He complained a little, but once we were on Old Money Road, his mood improved. He set his elbow out the truck window, leaned back, took a deep breath, and smiled. "This is where a man should be, Hiram. Working the earth. Planting, cultivating, harvesting. That's what made the South great, and that's what still sustains this country. Hillburn folk have worked the land for generations. Held on to it, expanded it, kept it to pass on to our children." He poked me in the shoulder. "Your daddy should have stayed here, son. He should be out there right now looking after Hillburn land and Hillburn crops."

When we reached the first of Grampa's fields, I steered the truck onto a dirt road and let it roll to a stop alongside the edge of the cotton rows. "Bet it feels good to be out here again, Grampa," I said.

"Yep," he said, but he looked sad again. "Feels real great to see the fruits of my labors. Awful glad you came, son. Awful glad . . ." He took a deep breath and sighed. "But I do wish Harlan were here too. You remind me of him, Hiram, now more than ever before. I miss my boy."

I knew Grampa wanted me to say that Dad missed him too, that he wanted to come to Greenwood and just couldn't get away from work, that someday we'd all be back here again. But it wasn't true, and Grampa would know it. I didn't want to talk or even think about Dad, so I didn't say anything.

We sat without talking for a while, watching the breeze stir the tops of the cotton plants. Finally, Grampa spoke. "You know, sometimes you wish you could go back and change things with people. I loved Harlan and treated him right, but somewhere he went haywire. Or *we* went haywire. Seemed to always get along with his mother, but soured on me when he turned twelve. That's when he started acting contrary, and nothing I did could shake it out of him. It got so I didn't even know how to talk to him anymore. Florence, God bless her, tried to help. Harlan'd listen to her. I know he loves the Delta—it's in his blood—but I've never understood why he wouldn't stay."

A tear ran down his cheek, but he ignored it. "It's damn hard being old and alone, Hiram," he said in a voice so soft, I could hardly hear him. "Too damn hard."

I felt a catch in my throat and a sadness that reached clear back to my childhood. I hadn't seen Grampa cry since that day Gramma died. More than anything, I wanted to hug him, to tell him things would be all right someday. My big old grandfather who had always been strong and loud and cheerful now seemed pitiful, sad, and hopeless. I wished he and Dad could talk, could be together again. I wanted him to be happy, but I didn't know how to make it happen. The only thing I could think to say was, "I'm sorry, Grampa. Really I am."

I couldn't tell if he heard me or not.

Nobody said anything for a while; then Grampa straightened up and cleared his throat. "Let's head on up through Money," he said, "and I'll show you how to find our old fishing hole on the Tallahatchie."

I started the truck and followed his directions up and down the dirt farm roads until we came to our fishing spot. From there we drove through a lot of Leflore County, not stopping anywhere, but driving past the fields of Grampa's friends and going through little towns where he'd done some business once or had a great meal or two. Seeing those familiar places brightened him up, and by the time we were headed back to Greenwood, he said, "Let's not go home just yet. Why don't we drive over to the county courthouse? I haven't been there in weeks, and I've got some business to tend to."

I drove us back through town and over the Yazoo on the Fulton Street Bridge and parked in front of the Leflore County Courthouse. Grampa couldn't wait to get out of the truck. "I wonder if Eddie Crisler is still working. C'mon, Hiram, and we'll wake the old devil up."

Mr. Crisler stood and smiled when Grampa and I came in. "Earl, you rascal," he said, "how've you been?"

"Been better," said Grampa. "You know about my stroke of bad luck." Both men laughed at his dumb joke, then started talking about fishing and folks in town and who'd died and who hadn't. When Mr. Crisler mentioned something about the Citizens' Councils, Grampa cleared his throat and looked my way.

"Hiram, Mr. Crisler and I have some serious business to tend to for the next little while." Just like old times, he reached into his pocket, pulled out a dime, and flipped it to me. "Why don't you run down the lobby and say hey to Mr. Paul. Bet he won't recognize you."

I strolled down the main lobby of the courthouse toward Mr. Paul's concessions stand. It had been seven years, almost half my life, since I'd been there, but nothing had changed. My footsteps echoed off the marble floor like they always had. Old Mr. Taylor, the security guard, still stood outside the courtroom door, and there in the middle of the main lobby was Mr. Paul's little stand, just as I remembered it. Mr. Paul looked the same, except he wasn't wearing dark glasses now, and as I got closer, I saw that he'd framed his Purple Heart medal from the war and hung it on the wall behind his stand.

When he heard my footsteps, he turned my way and smiled. "Can I help you?" he asked.

"Hey, Mr. Paul, it's me, Hiram Hillburn, back from Arizona to visit."

"Well, well, Hiram, how's the world been treating you? Better than it has your grampa, I hope."

"I've been missing Greenwood something awful," I said, "but Arizona's not all that bad. I've got two brothers and two sisters now."

"Isn't that something? Guess your folks are doing well and your daddy's happy."

"Yessir, he likes teaching at the college."

"Shame he's too busy to come back once in a while to visit old Earl. It was hard on him when ya'll moved away." Mr. Paul stepped back and sat on a stool behind the counter. "So what brings you in here today? Your grampa doing 'business' again?"

"Yessir, and he sent me down here with a dime. Have you got any cold root beer?"

He reached behind him into an ice chest, pulled out a bottle of Frosty Root Beer, opened it, and set it on the counter.

I snapped my dime on the counter top, and he picked it up and dropped it into his change tray. "Pleasure doing business with you, Hiram. You going to be in Greenwood long?"

"A couple of weeks, I guess. Dad says I've got to get back in time for school."

"You don't sound too happy about that."

"School's all right, but Grampa's been feeling pretty lonely, and I kind of wanted to help him get around as long as I can." I took a swig of root beer and asked, "So what's new in Greenwood?"

"Same old small-town things. Babies get born, old folks die. A few young kids run off and get married. Sitting here where I do all day, I hear most of what goes on. Lately, lots of folks have been pretty hot about school integration. Those fellows on the Supreme Court didn't make many friends down here."

"You think they're really going to integrate?"

"Over some folks' dead bodies, I'd say. Your grampa and his friends in the White Citizens' Council are pretty worked up over it. They're dead set on keeping the colored schools separate from the white. It's the 'way of the South' and all that."

"But don't Negroes want their own schools just like we do?"

"Ever been to a colored school, Hiram?"

"Nosir."

"I went to one once, before the war, to fix a plumbing leak they had in the colored elementary school. The building wasn't much more than a big shack. Kids didn't have any books that I could see. The school desks were older than I was. The principal told me that she'd been calling the county office about the water leak for four months before I finally showed up, and all that time the school'd been without water."

"How come you didn't go sooner?"

"Hiram, I went the day after the county office called me about it. Nobody cared that the colored school didn't have any water. So, how'd you like to go to a school with outdoor privies, no books, rickety old desks, and no water most of the time?"

"But how do you know that's not just one school? Other colored schools might be better."

"This is Mississippi, Hiram. The South. Most colored schools are lucky to see ten cents of every school tax dollar. The rest goes to the white schools, the kind you went to when you lived here. Jim Crow laws keep things separate not equal, and if those White Citizens' Councils have anything to say about it, Jim Crow will rule the South until doomsday."

"And what's wrong with that? What's wrong with people keeping to their own kind? Grampa used to say that's the way God wants it."

"Hiram"—Mr. Paul's face turned serious—"maybe God put different kinds of people on earth so we could all learn to get along. Ever think about that?" Mr. Paul turned toward the sound of footsteps coming our way.

"You getting this boy what he needs?" It was Grampa.

"That you, Earl? You've been away too long. Guess it took your grandson visiting to pry you out of that big old easy chair."

Grampa laughed. "That's just about right. It's been good having the boy around again; he makes getting out a heck of a lot more fun."

They talked for a while about Mr. Paul's children, the weather, and local politics, but nobody said anything about integration or the Citizens' Councils. Just polite, empty talk.

Pretty soon Mr. Paul said he had to close up shop because his wife would be coming by to take him home. We said good-bye and went home to dinner.

Ruthanne fed us like kings again. Grampa ate well but didn't say much. All the driving around and visiting we'd done must've taken a lot out of him, because as soon as dinner was over, he went straight to bed.

The house was quiet and dark when I went upstairs. I wasn't all that tired, but that's not why I had a hard time sleeping. Thinking about how lonely Grampa was made me sad, especially because there wasn't a thing I could do about it, and because I knew that unless a bolt of lightning struck Dad, there'd be no way he'd offer to patch things up with Grampa.

And I was thinking about what Mr. Paul had said. In Tempe, segregation never seemed to be a big deal; in Greenwood things were different. It wasn't just the schools; restaurants, movie theaters, stores, even the neighborhoods were divided into white or colored. And the white places were always one hundred times nicer. The Jim Crow laws kept the Negroes pretty much stuck where they were—with no hope of things ever getting better. Their future must have seemed hopeless.

Then I thought about Emmett. He seemed like a regular kid, even though his skin wasn't the same color as mine. I couldn't imagine him going to a colored school, and maybe in Chicago he didn't have to. Maybe there things were different. Maybe like Mr. Paul'd said, God didn't want to keep us separate. He wanted us to get along. Maybe—and this was a surprising thought—Dad's ideas weren't so crazy after all.

I'd have to think about that for a while. I could see where segregation wasn't very fair, but it wasn't the same as something like the Nazis killing all those Jews. It seemed to me that Negroes weren't really being hurt; it was just the way things were, and I couldn't see why people like Dad and Mr. Paul got so worked up over it, especially when it had nothing to do with them.

Dad, Grampa, Mr. Paul, and Emmett stayed on my mind for quite a while, but none of them seemed to be suffering. Things couldn't be as bad as either Grampa or Dad made them out to be.

As it got later, I found something better to think about: Naomi Rydell. When would I see her? Far as I was concerned, the sooner the better.

CHAPTER 8

R. C. Rydell had gotten bigger. I ran into him Tuesday downtown at the P&S Drugstore, where he was slouched against the front wall looking bored and smoking filterless Viceroys. He stood at least six feet tall and had round powerful shoulders and thick forearms. A jagged line ran across his right cheek, and his eyebrows were crisscrossed with thin white scars.

When he saw me, he flicked a smoldering cigarette butt in my direction. "What in hell are you doin' here? We figured when ya'll run out to Arizona, we'd never see you again." He grinned and shoved me back a step. "Shoot, Hiram, you done grown up. How long's it been?"

"Seven years. We left in '48."

"Wasn't much after that I quit school. Wastin' my time there, Pa said. He got me a man's job unloadin' freight barges that come down the Yazoo. Didn't need no schoolin' for that. So, whatcha doin' nowadays?"

"Still in high school back in Arizona. I'll be in eleventh grade next month."

"Figures," R.C. said with a snort. "You always was a sisbaby. I'll bet school suits you just fine. So, how come you're in Greenwood? You runnin' from the law?"

"Naw, just visiting Grampa. He's been sick, you know, and none of us have been back to see him since we moved."

"Yeah, I heard he was a cripple or somethin' now. Too bad, 'cause he's always had things squared away pretty good, if you ask me."

I really didn't feel like asking R.C. anything, so I stepped around him and reached for the drugstore door. "Good seeing you, R.C., but I've got to be getting Grampa's medicine."

R.C. moved aside to let me pass but put a hand on my shoulder to stop me. "Tell you what, Hiram, we ain't got no barges comin' down for another couple days, so why don't we go fishin' tomorrow? I can see if you learned anythin' since you been in Arizona. It'll be like old times."

Old times with R.C. hadn't always been fun, but maybe fishing wouldn't be so bad; he was eighteen and probably had mellowed some since we were kids. And maybe he'd let me know what Naomi was doing, and if there was some way I could see her. "Yeah, okay. If he hasn't already loaned it out to one of his friends, we can probably use Grampa's truck and drive out to the Tallahatchie instead of walking down the Yazoo. Last week he showed me how to get to his favorite fishing hole out there."

R.C. leaned back against the storefront and lit another Viceroy. "I'll come by in the mornin', and maybe I'll be able to steal a little of Pa's beer to keep us from dyin' of thirst while we's fishin'."

"No need for any beer, especially in the morning." I knew R.C. and beer would be a bad combination. "Lemonade'll do me fine. I'll bring a thermos of it."

"I shoulda figured you'd be a sisbaby who don't smoke or drink. Don't matter. I'll bring my beer, you bring your lemonade. We'll have us some fun." He took a long drag on his cigarette and let the smoke drift out his nostrils. "See you round, Hiram."

That night Grampa said we could use his pickup truck. "From what I hear lately, it'll do R.C. some good going fishing with a nice boy like you. If nothing else, it'll keep him out of mischief. Won't hurt you any either, Hiram; you need to get out with some boys your own age. Hanging around with an old man like me all the time can't be much fun. Just make sure you bring us back some catfish. Ruthanne can put together some hush puppies and fry up those fish, and we'll have us a meal you won't forget."

Ruthanne insisted on fixing me a lunch to take along with my lemonade, and when I picked up the canvas bag on my way out the next morning, it felt as jam-packed as anything Gramma had ever made. She didn't have to do that, I knew, but that's how Ruthanne was. It felt good to leave the house on a fishing trip with enough lunch for me and R.C. Just like old times.

By the time I had my fishing gear in the back of the truck and my lunch sack on the front seat, R.C. showed up, looking ragged and red-eyed. "You okay?" I asked when he climbed into the truck.

"Had a long night," he said. "Stuff a sisbaby like you wouldn't know nothin' about. I'll be fine by the time we're out at the river."

"Hey, R.C., how's Naomi doing? I haven't had a chance to talk to her since I got back."

He looked surprised; then his eyebrows arched up and he grinned. "Oh, yeah, I forgot 'bout you two. Regular little lovebirds when you was here before. I shoulda told her you was back in Greenwood, but I got in kinda late and Pa was on a bender. She's smart enough to make herself scarce when Pa's rippin'."

"But she's doing all right; I mean, she's okay?"

"Lookit here, sisbaby, I take care of my little sister, not that she needs it much anymore, but long as I'm around, don't nobody hurt her. Course, I keep the Romeos away too, but in your case, old buddy, I'll make an exception. Naomi always was sweet on you." He leaned back and looked me over. "But I don't know what she's gonna think of the growed up and ugly version of you."

"When you get home, tell her I said hey, will you? Let her know I'm in town, and maybe sometime we can—"

R.C. held up a hand to stop me. "Hold on a minute. I said

I'd let you see my sister, but I didn't say I'd make all your damn appointments. You work out your own matchmaking, Hiram Hillburn. If Naomi wants to see you, she'll see you. She don't, she won't. And if that happens to be the case, you'd dadgum better not be botherin' her about it.

"Enough about your love life; let's get out of here." He held up a brown paper sack. "Got us—sorry, I got *me* six bottles of Pa's beer to help get through the day. Good thing you don't drink, Hiram boy, 'cause these six will be barely enough for me." He set the beer alongside the bulging lunch sack on the seat between us. "Whatcha got here?"

"Ruthanne packed us a lunch. Looks like we'll have plenty."

R.C. didn't grab the sack like I'd expected him to. "Ruthanne that nigger girl your granddaddy got workin' for him?"

"Ever since Gramma died, and she's a great cook. Just as good as Gramma ever was."

He pushed the bag away. "Be a cold day in hell 'fore I eat nigger food. Don't matter how good it is. Never did understand your granddaddy on that. He's right-thinkin' in most ways, but he lets a nigger in and out of his house like she's family." He smirked and raised an eyebrow. "But who knows? Maybe she's been doin' a whole lot more than just cookin' and cleanin'."

"You're nuts, R.C." Right then I wanted to pop him in the jaw. "Grampa's not like that, and neither is Ruthanne. Just can it for a while, will you?"

He looked surprised, then he grinned and reached in his shirt pocket and pulled out a cigarette. "Looks like Arizona's turned you into a nigger-lover." He lit the cigarette and tossed the match out the window. "Fine. Just fine. I don't like talkin' about coloreds anyway. You're drivin'. Let's go get us some fish."

I backed out the driveway and turned onto Cotton Street just as Ronnie Remington was crossing in front of us on his way to the courthouse. He moved slowly, his head down, oblivious to us. R.C. reached over and pounded the truck horn.

Ronnie's head snapped up, his eyes huge, and he stopped dead in the road in front of us like an old cow caught in the glare of a car's headlights. R.C. honked the horn twice more, then leaned out his window, pounded the side of the door with his arm, and yelled, "Move your fat ass, you old queer!" Ronnie looked terrified when he recognized R.C., and he wobbled as quickly as he could to the sidewalk while R.C. whooped and catcalled. Ronnie stood frozen and pale as we drove past, and R.C. laughed like a crazy man.

I couldn't help laughing too. "Geez, R.C., you almost gave him a heart attack. I thought he was going to jump out of his shoes."

"Yeah, them old Remingtons is always good for a laugh. A couple years ago, every time I'd catch me a carp, I'd slice its gut open and leave it in their mailbox."

"No kidding? I bet they hated getting mail."

"That's nothing. Last year I got so fed up seein' them two

fairies walkin' around town that I offered Ralph a ride one day when I had Pa's truck, and instead of takin' him home, I headed out of town. We drove ten minutes before he even said anything."

"What'd he do?"

"What could the old weirdo do? I could bust him in half if I wanted. Anyways, I stop the truck and tell him I like him so much, I want all his clothes. He stared at me with his mouth hangin' open like some stupid fish. 'Get out and gimme your clothes,' I told him. He just sat there like an idiot, so I slapped him around a little. He started moanin' and cryin' and finally got out. Made him strip naked. Boy, was that a sorry sight. If I had a body like his, I'd shoot myself. Felt so sorry for him, I tossed his shoes back before I drove off."

This didn't sound funny anymore. "You left him there? Naked?"

"Didn't hurt him none. I saw him around town again a couple days later. Some sappy old farmer probably picked him up and give him a feedbag or something to cover up with. You know how people around here put up with them Remingtons."

R.C. hadn't changed, and I would have turned around and gone back home if I could have thought up a good excuse. I didn't say anything more to R.C., and after a few minutes, he leaned his head against the door and fell asleep.

I felt lousy the rest of the way to the Tallahatchie. R. C. Rydell was one screwed up kid, and for the life of me, I couldn't understand why he—or anyone—would enjoy making other people miserable. Maybe R.C. was so miserable himself that he was always looking for somebody or something he could make worse off than he was. But he always took it too far; it's one thing to have a little fun with someone, teasing and stuff like that, but R.C. was just plain mean.

And to tell you the truth, he scared the crap out of me.

When I finally parked the truck at the clearing not far from Grampa's fishing hole, I was feeling better. The lush green of the Delta and the heavy damp smell from the fields helped me get my mind on something other than R.C.'s bullying.

R.C. woke up when I opened my door. "Where are we?" He looked around, confused.

"Don't know for sure. A few miles from Money. Grampa and I used to come here all the time when I was a kid. It's a good spot. Anyway, you can sleep some more if you want. I'm heading to the river to get settled."

"Good idea." R.C. leaned his head back, closed his eyes, and waved me away. "I'll come down after I get me some more beauty rest."

I grabbed the lunch sack, picked up my fishing gear, and worked my way down to the river's edge. I was glad to be alone. The morning sky was clear blue, the grass damp and dew streaked. The sound of the wind in the trees and the flow of the Tallahatchie made me want to hurry up and find a shady spot to take a nap. I followed the narrow path parallel to the river for a few minutes until I recognized a place under an old cypress tree. I tucked the lunch bag up against the tree trunk, baited my hook, and cast out into the middle of the river. Then I sat down against the tree and watched the water.

It felt great to be fishing again, but it didn't seem right without Grampa. He needed to be there, because even though I loved the Delta countryside, that wasn't what I'd been missing. What I really wanted was to relive some of my favorite experiences, experiences that always included Grampa. When I was little, he'd taught me to fish somewhere around here; I'd never had a bad day with Grampa while we were fishing, never saw him lose his temper, never had him get mad when I snagged my line or lost a fish. You know, he probably didn't care at all about catching fish back then: He took me fishing because he enjoyed spending time with me.

I wondered about Dad and Grampa. Had Dad ever stood here with Grampa's arms around him helping him cast a line? Had they ever told stories, joked, and splashed together on the riverbank while they cleaned the day's catch?

Suddenly, it mattered a lot that they had. As much as I loved my good times with Grampa, I didn't want them to be a substitute for what he should have done with Dad when he was a boy. My childhood memories with Grampa might be something, maybe one of the only things, Dad and I had in common, and I made up my mind that when I got back to Tempe, I'd ask Dad about it.

All my serious thinking ended when a rock ricocheted

off the tree just above my head. "Woo-ee, Hiram boy! You in a trance or what? I coulda snuck up on you, slit your throat, swiped your lunch, and drove away in your truck without you even knowin' it." R.C. tramped down to the riverbank. "You been drinkin', boy?"

"Just thinking. That's one of the things I like about being here."

"No wonder you never catch no fish." R.C. set his pole down to bait his hook. "There's got to be somebody payin' attention at your end of that pole, or those fish'll strip your hook clean." He pulled a bottle of beer from his bag. "Let me show you how this is supposed to be done, boy. First, you got to wet your whistle. The faster, the better." He popped the cap off the bottle with his pocketknife, then chugged the entire beer without hardly taking a breath. "Ahh, that's better." He tossed the empty bottle into the river. "Now, fish, look out. I'm a-comin' for you."

R.C. walked a few yards downstream and cast his line into the river. Minutes later I heard him whoop. "Got me one! Hoo-boy, this is gonna be a good day!" He pulled his stringer from his pocket and strung the fish on it. "Tell you one thing, Hiram, your granddaddy sure knows where the fish are." The rest of the morning went like that, R.C. guzzling beer and pulling in fish. By noon he had a stringer full of fish and a belly full of beer; he was red-faced and a little unsteady when he trudged over and dropped down alongside me. "All that fishin's made me hungry, Hiram boy. Whatcha got for lunch?"

I almost reminded him of what he'd said about Ruth-anne's food, but figured I didn't want him to knock my teeth down my throat. "Help yourself to whatever's in there. We got plenty."

He pulled out two sandwiches, tore the wax paper off one, and tossed the other to me. "Eat up, boy. Can't work on no empty stomach." He set the lunch sack between us, and we dug in. I hadn't realized how hungry I was, and, of course, Ruthanne had packed us a sack lunch better than most people's suppers. We had lots more than we could eat.

While we ate, R.C. talked about how many fish he'd caught, his work down on the docks, and some raunchy stuff about girls he'd known. I knew most of his stories were a bunch of baloney, but it was mostly harmless stuff, so I didn't sweat it.

I hadn't slept much the night before, and Ruthanne's lunch combined with the heavy afternoon air hit me like a sleeping drug. R.C. was yawning too, so I said, "No place better in the Delta for a quiet nap than right in the shade of one of these willow trees. After we wake up, we can decide if we want to fish some more or head back into town."

R.C. settled into a shady spot a few yards downstream and was snoring in minutes. I didn't last much longer.

I don't know how long I'd been asleep when I jerked awake. It took a moment for my head to clear, but when it did, I heard splashing and laughter from upstream.

Thirty or forty yards from us where the bank sloped gradually into shallow water, four Negro boys were horsing around in the water. Dressed only in cutoff pants, all of them were soaking wet. They were playing some sort of three on one, where three of them ganged up on one to dunk him.

I watched them wrestle, splash, and laugh. They were really having a good time, splashing their way downstream, and when they were close enough, I recognized one of them. Emmett wasn't the biggest kid, but he was the best at playing their game. He was as wet as any of them, but he was always one of the dunkers and never the dunkee.

A couple of the boys saw me sitting in the shade of that tree, and as soon as they did, they stopped dead, pointed at me, and motioned to the others to head back upstream. Emmett didn't want to stop, and he was the last one to see me. He held one hand over his eyes to shade his view, then he recognized me, waved, and started walking toward me. The other boys grabbed him. "You crazy?" one said. "Let's get outta here 'fore there's trouble."

"Trouble?" Emmett waved a hand at them. "That's one of my friends. The old Tallahatchie lifeguard. He ain't no trouble."

"He's *white*," hissed another one of the boys. "That's trouble enough."

"D-d-didn't I tell you I had white friends up in Chicago?" He slogged through the shallow water and onto the riverbank.

I wanted to keep him as far away from R.C. as I could, so I jumped up and met him at the bank. When he saw me coming, he turned to his friends and said, "See? Told you we was friends."

"Hey, Emmett," I said, "what you all up to?"

"Just goofing around with some of my cousins. Too hot to be anywhere b-b-but in the water. What're you d-d-doing, fishing or sleeping?"

"Little of both, I guess. Ruthanne's lunch and this old Mississippi sun pretty much wiped me out."

"Lunch?" Emmett's face lit up. "We're starving; got anything left?"

Emmett's friends had stayed behind him a ways in the water, close enough to hear, but far enough away to escape if they had to. "Aw, geez, Emmett," said one, "let's just get on home. No need to be hanging round here."

Emmett waved a hand behind his back and said without even turning around, "You all go on if you want to. I'm gonna get me something to eat."

The boys didn't move. "Told you," said one. "He's crazy." They all laughed and splashed water at him.

"Wait here," I told Emmett. "I'll go grab my lunch sack and you all can have whatever's left in it."

I started back to the tree where I'd left my stuff, but Emmett followed me. "Shoot," he said, "I d-don't want to stand out there with that old sun b-beating down on me eating my lunch. No snakes up around that tree, is there?"

When they saw him follow me up on the shore, Emmett's friends whooped and laughed. "Go, Bobo!" one yelled. "Go, you crazy boy!"

I turned around and faced him. "Look, it'd be better if you stayed down there. My friend's sleeping over there, and he probably doesn't want to get woke up."

"Hey, any friend of yours is a friend of mine," Emmett said with a grin. "Now let's see what Ruthanne p-p-packed us for lunch." He wasn't going to listen, so I figured the best thing to do was to give him my lunch and get him out of there. I handed him the sack as his cousins kept laughing and yelling at him. He ignored them.

Unfortunately, R.C. didn't.

He came up from behind and shoved me out of the way so he was facing Emmett himself. "What the hell's goin' on here?" he said slowly. R.C.'s face was red and he smelled like stale beer. "Looks like you caught yourself one helluva colored fish, Hiram." He snorted through his nose, cleared his throat, and spit at Emmett's feet. "Too bad it's a trash fish. You'll have to throw him back."

I had a feeling something real ugly was about to happen. For some reason, maybe because he didn't know R.C., Emmett didn't seem worried at all, even though his cousins had backed away without making a sound.

"Let's not have any trouble, R.C.," I said. "I was just giving Emmett our leftovers."

"Givin' our lunch to a *nigger*? You must be as crazy as your pa was. I'd just as soon throw our food to the fish as see it go to waste on this trash." He snatched the sack out of Emmett's hand. "You leave this be, Hiram, or I'll fix you, your grampa, and your whole family real good, I swear to God."

R.C. glared at me with pure hatred, and I backed off, afraid to do anything more.

"Hey," Emmett chuckled nervously. Finally, he must have gotten some good sense, "I d-d-didn't mean nothing. My friend here was sharing his lunch, and—"

R.C. shoved him in the chest. "White folk don't share nothin' with colored, boy. Nothin'."

Emmett staggered back a step but didn't shut up. "Look, I didn't mean anything by it, b-b-but he did say we could have that sack. Why d-don't you just let me have it, and we'll get out of here."

"Don't you hear, boy, or are you just tired of breathing?" R.C. threw the lunch sack down and kicked it out of the way. "I've had enough of your uppityness." He lunged forward and grabbed Emmett in a headlock. "You so hungry, I'll feed you lunch." R.C. dragged him over to where'd he'd been fishing. Emmett struggled and complained at first, but R.C. tightened his grip around Emmett's neck, and he quieted down, half scrambling, half being dragged behind R.C.

When they got to the riverbank, R.C. threw Emmett on the ground and held him there with one knee on his chest. He reached over and pulled his fish line out of the river and laid the fish across Emmett's bare stomach. When a fish twitched, Emmett flexed upward and tried to twist away, but R.C.'s knee kept him pinned. "Lemme go!" Emmett yelled. "Get off me."

"Lunchtime, boy," R.C. said as he pulled his pocketknife from his pants. He opened the blade and held it over Emmett.

Emmett froze.

"C'mon, R.C.," I yelled, "cut it out."

He waved his knife at me. "I warned you once, Hiram. Ain't gonna do it again." Then he smiled. "'Sides, I ain't doin' nothin' but givin' this uppity black boy his lunch. You hold still, boy," he said to Emmett, "I'd hate to see you get hurt by accident."

R.C. swung his leg over and sat on Emmet's stomach, then he slid the fish up to Emmett's neck. His knife blade flashed in the sun.

"Come on, get off," Emmett yelled as he bucked upward, trying to throw R.C. off, but R.C. was too big for him.

"Hang on, boy, you don't want me to drop this knife on some vital part, do you? Just set still while I get you some lunch." He pulled the largest fish off the stringer and held it in one hand with its white belly facing up. "Carp. You coloreds love carp." He stuck his blade into the tail end of the fish and cut up to its head, letting the blood drip onto Emmett's chest and face. He gagged and yelled for help, but R.C. held him.

R.C. threw his knife into the ground just inches from Emmett's face. Emmett didn't move, didn't yell. His eyes looked huge. Then R.C. scraped the guts out of the fish and shoved them in Emmett's face.

Emmett thrashed and twisted his head from side to side, and R.C. threw the fish carcass into the river so he could use one hand to hold Emmett's head still and the other to hold the guts over Emmett's mouth and nose.

"R.C., he can't breathe," I yelled. "You're going to kill him!"

He ignored me, and when Emmett finally opened his mouth for air, R.C. shoved the guts in and rolled off Emmett, laughing. "You wasn't as hungry as you thought, boy," he said as Emmett retched and rolled on the ground. R.C. shook the blood from his hands onto Emmett. "Guess fresh carp don't much agree with you after all. That be the case, you best learn not to be so uppity around white folks, and you'd damn well better not be comin' around here askin' for any food again. Seems to me you don't like what we got to offer."

Emmett knelt on all fours, coughing and spitting. When he caught his breath, he turned and glared at R.C., and then at me before sliding into the shallow edge of the river and wading back to his cousins. They hadn't moved since R.C. woke up.

R.C. picked up his pocketknife, wiped the blade on his pants leg, folded it closed, and shoved it into his pocket. "Let's get out of here, Hiram. I'm done fishin'."

He picked up his stuff and headed back up the path to the truck. I stayed behind, sick to my stomach, embarrassed, and scared. Emmett and his cousins waded upstream with Emmett walking between two of them, leaning heavily on their shoulders. I wanted to say something, to yell that I was sorry, that I thought R.C. was evil and messed up, but they were too far to hear by then. Besides, I'd had my chance to do something, but all I'd done was watch R.C. humiliate that boy.

I felt dirty and weak.

And ashamed.

CHAPTER 9

During supper that night I felt so lousy about what R.C. had done that I could hardly face Ruthanne. Grampa could tell I was upset, and before I could slip upstairs to sulk in my room, he said, "Hiram, let's go set in the living room and you can tell me what's eating you. Ever since you got home from fishing, you've looked more miserable than a crawdad in a stew pot."

Frankly, I was glad for the chance to unload my feelings on Grampa, and he let me ramble about what had happened. I didn't get into all the gory stuff, but I did tell him that R. C. Rydell had done some awful things to a Negro boy while we were fishing. I could barely keep my voice from shaking.

"And the worst thing, Grampa, was that I just stood there. I could've pulled him off. I should've done something, but

I didn't know what to do." I felt my face turn red. "Truth is, I was scared."

"R.C. didn't do any permanent damage to the boy, just a little roughhousing that went too far. Besides, Hiram, boys like R.C. are as unpredictable as a mad dog; if you'd've gotten in his way, he might have ripped into you."

"But I should have done *something*. You should've seen how that boy looked at me when he left. He thought I was his friend."

"That's where he made his first mistake. Coloreds around here know better than to push themselves on white folks. There is no friendship between whites and coloreds, never should be, never will be. Even a fool oughtta known that."

"R.C. wasn't just acting unfriendly, Grampa; he was torturing him. It was crazy. Why would anybody act like that?"

"No explaining some people," Grampa said. "There are some ignorant white trash peckerwoods here in the Delta who are just plain mean. Maybe they've got things bad. Maybe they're mad about something. Maybe they can't hold their liquor. You can't understand them, son, and it's no use even trying."

"Should I tell the sheriff?"

Grampa shook his head. "I'm sure Sheriff Smith knows all about R. C. Rydell. That boy's been in and out of trouble his whole life. From what I hear, most of it's just dumb old peckerwood things like bullying people, swearing in public, boozing. But one thing's sure: He doesn't have the brains or the gumption to do anything much worse than what he did today. I don't approve of what he did, but you also got to remember, Hiram, this is the Mississippi Delta. Sounds to me like that colored boy just didn't have any sense. R.C.'s no good, and I'm damn sorry for what happened, but that boy brought trouble on himself."

I didn't know what to think, and I didn't want to talk to Grampa any longer, so I said good night and went upstairs to my room. Some of what Grampa said about R.C. made sense, but I couldn't think of anything anybody could do to deserve getting treated the way Emmett had been. Why had R.C. been so hateful to a kid he didn't even know? And what if lots of people like R.C. existed? What if they all got together?

They'd be dangerous to almost everyone, not just to Negroes.

Back in Arizona, I'd heard about how the Mormons had been chased out of most places they had lived until they'd finally settled in Utah, a desert nobody wanted. It was hard to believe that Americans could be that cruel to other people just because of religion, or race, or anything. The Nazi slaughter of the Jews, that seemed different—and worse. For one, it was an ocean away, foreigners hurting and killing other foreigners, and the Nazis weren't Americans; they didn't have the principles of freedom and democracy that we had. Maybe in a way, they just didn't know any better, or maybe old Hitler was just able to pull off mass hypnosis or something.

And maybe that's why Dad acted so crazy about the

South and segregation. Maybe he realized that bullies would always find somebody to pick on, if not the Negroes, then somebody else.

And I didn't want it to be me or anybody I loved.

In fact, I didn't want it to be anybody at all.

My head was so jammed with troubles that night that I could hardly keep it still on my pillow; plenty of my restlessness was because of what R.C. had done, but a whole lot of my tossing and turning came from my wondering if maybe Dad wasn't so crazy after all.

Grampa claimed he was feeling better, but his skin stayed gray and loose, and he hardly ever showed the passion for things that he used to when I was little. I tried to talk him into going fishing once in a while, but he said he didn't think he'd have the energy to reel in anything bigger than a minnow. Normally, I would have been bored, but I knew I wasn't going to be in Greenwood much longer, so I didn't mind spending time with Grampa. He still seemed lonely, and sometimes I worried about what he'd do when I was gone. Except for sitting around the house, checking on his land, and doing business at the courthouse, the only thing Grampa did that wasn't just regular living was his work on the White Citizens' Council. He never talked to me about what exactly he did, but I figured he was some kind of big shot on the Council; some nights two or three men would come over to talk to Grampa about what was going on. Twice since I came to Greenwood, he'd left at night for

Council meetings and came back late, long after I was asleep. I figured it was boring political stuff he was working at, probably had something to do with battling desegregation and all that. Seeing him so involved reminded me of Dad: all worked up and smack in the middle of some issue.

Thursday I stayed close to home, spending as much time with Grampa as I could, and it was like old times: After Ruthanne's breakfast Grampa and I got into the pickup and drove over to the courthouse and then out to the fields. We didn't stay in either place very long, and ended up at the River Café by noon. After lunch we went home so he could take a nap. When he woke up, he sat in his favorite chair and read Civil War history books until Ruthanne had supper ready. After supper he went back to the living room to read *The Greenwood Commonwealth,* and we talked about the news, his childhood, and whatever else he felt like talking about. A knock at the door interrupted us, and Grampa answered it: Some guy came by wanting to borrow the truck. "Key's are in it," Grampa told him. "Just make sure it's got some gas left when you're done." He walked back to his chair smiling; I could tell it made him feel good to help out his neighbors.

Later that evening some men picked Grampa up for another Council meeting. For a while after he left, I sat in the living room reading the newspaper and listening to the radio. The man who had borrowed the truck had already returned it, so I thought about taking it and cruising Greenwood, but there wasn't a whole lot to see in Greenwood at night. Besides, there really was only one person I wanted to see, even though I wasn't sure how I could see her or if she'd want to see me.

By 10:00 I was bored and restless, so I went for a walk. Greenwood's dead quiet at night, and as I walked along River Road, the only thing I heard except for the buzz of the summer locusts and the sound of an occasional car or truck, was the soft flow of the Yazoo River down below the sidewalk. After a few blocks I turned left on Fulton Street and walked onto the bridge that crossed the river.

Halfway across stood a girl looking over the railing. The dim streetlight at one end didn't do much to break up the shadows that blanketed most of the bridge, but as I got closer, I could see that she had blonde hair and was staring at the dark water flowing beneath us.

My chest got tight when I recognized her. She didn't move as I approached, and I had to work to take a breath before I spoke. "Naomi? What are you doing out here?"

She answered without looking up, without a trace of surprise. "I'm lookin' at the river, Hiram Hillburn, and thinkin' about an old friend."

I stood next to her. "Been here long?"

"Just every night since I heard you were back in Greenwood." She bumped her shoulder into mine and turned her head so I could see her. Wow, she was even prettier than she was when we were kids. "Where have you been? Did living in Arizona make you forget your Mississippi friends?"

"Naomi, I—"

"Don't go fretting about it, Hiram." She smiled and nudged me with her hip. "I'm just teasin'."

"Really, I've wanted to see you and all, but I've been pretty busy since I got here, and I wasn't sure, you know, how you'd feel if I just showed up one afternoon."

"I would've felt right fine about it. It's not like I get many visitors out to the house. R.C. and Pa make dang sure of that, believe me. You of all people oughtta know that I'd be hoping you'd show up, but I knew your grampa'd been sick and all, and that you were tending him. Still, you can't blame me for wishing you'd come and see me. It's been an awful long time, Hiram." She spoke without sadness, and seeing her smile and hearing her beautiful Southern voice made me glad I'd come to the bridge that night.

"I have seen R.C. a few times, and I asked about you."

"R.C." Naomi rolled her eyes. "I'd like to wring his neck. Do you know that he waited two whole days before he even told me you were in town? Not that I see him much anyways, with him working days and tomcattin' around at night, but he should've been a little more thoughtful, and I let him know it too." Naomi was the only person alive who could scold R. C. Rydell and get away with it.

"He hasn't changed much, has he? I mean, he's bigger and all, but he's still R.C." I almost told her what he had done to Emmett at the river, but I decided bad news about her brother wouldn't do her any good. She already knew—better than anybody—the kind of guy he was.

"I wish he'd turn over a new leaf," she said. "He used to be just ornery, but lately he's been worse than that, almost like he's trying to get into trouble or trying to prove something. Sometimes I worry about him, Hiram, that he's looking for something he's never going to find."

Enough about R.C. I'd had all I wanted of him lately. "So, how's your dad doing?"

Naomi blinked when I said "dad," but her expression didn't change. "Fine. Same as ever. Everything's just fine at home." Her voice was hard, firm. I knew she didn't want to talk about her father, so I just stood there looking at her, looking at the Yazoo, and neither one of us talked.

Finally, she spoke again. "Hiram, you ever want to get away? You know, just take a break from everything?"

"Are you kidding? I've been trying to get back to Greenwood for seven years. Sometimes my dad really bugs me, and for the last few years, it seems like all we do is fight, so I couldn't wait to get away from home."

"And are you glad you did? I mean, has it helped any?"

"I don't know. At first it was fun, riding the train alone and all, visiting with Grampa, seeing places and people I knew when I was a kid. But it hasn't been all fun; some things have changed around here, at least they seem like they've changed to me. I'm not sure how I feel about that. Kind of disappointed, I guess."

"Have I changed?" She smiled, her voice teasing me. "Are you disappointed?"

"You've changed, all right, but believe me, I'm not disappointed."

"Good." She looped her arm through mine. "I'll let you keep talking then."

I remembered why I had always loved being around her. Naomi was so easy to be with, so comfortable. Most good-looking girls made me nervous, but being with Naomi seemed like the most natural thing in the world. "Anyway, I've been thinking about things, about my dad and my grampa. Those two never did get along, just like me and Dad don't get along. But, I don't know. Some stuff that's happened down here has made me wonder about Dad, kind of helped me think about him in a different way."

Naomi leaned her head against my shoulder and sighed. "You know, I'm dying to leave, even if it's only for a little while, but I'm not like you. There's no place for me to go. R.C. can be a real headache when he's around, but at least he looks out for me, always has. Lately, though, I can feel him pulling away, and I don't know what I'm going to do when he finally leaves. He's working, and feeling more like a man every day, ready to be on his own. Pa can't see it, and he still treats R.C. like a kid, and sometimes, boy, do they battle." Her voice grew soft and sad again. "It's hard to take, awful hard to take."

I slid my arm around her shoulders and hugged her. "I'm sorry, Naomi, truly sorry."

She hugged me back, hard, but her body felt soft against mine and her hair smelled fresh, like river water.

After supper Friday night Grampa was reading the news-paper, and I was out on the back porch hoping for a cool breeze. I'd been thinking a lot about Dad and Grampa, about how the three of us were connected even though on the surface we seemed to be pretty disconnected. My life felt like it had been tied into a giant knot, one that would take a long time to untangle. I was looking forward to going back to Tempe, because maybe I could finally talk to Dad, and we could start undoing some of the snags we'd gotten all caught up in.

While I was sitting on the porch steps, R.C. crashed through the back bushes. My stomach tightened as he flicked his cigarette into the grass and sat down next to me.

"Ain't seen you round town for a while, Hiram."

"Been spending most of my time with Grampa. That's what I came here for."

"We sure had us a good time fishin' Wednesday. You remember that?"

"Only thing I remember is you torturing that kid." Even though R.C. scared the heck out of me, I had to say something. Maybe he'd break my neck right there, maybe he wouldn't, but I knew I wouldn't be able to sleep that night if I didn't finally stand up to R. C. Rydell. "And I want to tell you something, R.C.: I'm never letting you—or anyone—do stuff like that around me again."

R.C. looked surprised. "What are you talkin' about, Hiram? All's I remember is that you and me went fishing on the Tallahatchie, caught us some fish, ate us some lunch, took a nap, and headed home. Nothing else. Pa even remembers that string of fish I brung home."

"Yeah, well, I remember something sick. Something wrong."

"Is that right? Well, Hiram boy, don't go forgettin' that you was there the whole time, and you're just as much to blame for anything sick or wrong that might've happened."

"What are you talking about?"

"Sheriff Smith come round askin' questions yesterday, stuff about some black boy from Chicago. Old Mose Wright, the kid's uncle, complained that a couple local guys had been pickin' on the boy, and he remembered that one of 'em's name was R.C. Course, the sheriff don't put much stock in some strange nigger's complainin', but he said it was his sworn duty to check out the boy's story. I told him I didn't know no strange niggers, and he knew I steered clear of colored folks anyhow.

"'Just checking,' he told me. 'Just making sure no peckerwoods round here start any illegal violence.' He told me to stay out of trouble and then left, and I been wonderin' if he come talk to you yet."

I shook my head.

"Well, if he does, just you make sure you get your story straight. We don't want to be confusin' poor old Sheriff Smith."

"Look, R.C., if you're asking me to lie, forget it. I haven't seen Sheriff Smith, and I don't plan on seeing him, but if he comes around asking questions, I'm going to tell the truth."

R.C. swore and jumped to his feet. "You little sisbaby! I shoulda knowed you'd get all cry-ey over that colored boy."

He looked mad enough to chew tar, and just when I expected an uppercut to my jaw, he smiled. "But hell, it don't matter none. Smith'll believe me over you. You ain't been around here for years anyway, and you're goin' back home pretty soon." He patted me on the shoulder. "Guess I worried you over nothin', Hiram boy."

He lit a Viceroy, and I got up to go back inside. "What's your hurry? Don't you want to sit around and visit with an old pal?"

"You got that right, R.C."

"Well then, I'm glad I came to say good-bye. One other thing. You hear about that trouble up in Money a couple days ago?"

"Trouble you're in the middle of?"

"Me?" R.C. grinned. "No, not me. Least not yet. Naw, it's nigger trouble. Some strange nigger messed with a white woman up to Bryant's store."

"What do you mean 'messed with'? He raped a white woman?"

"Naw, but the boy don't know his place. Folks are sayin' he talked ugly and whistled at her. A married woman, even. The lady's husband was pretty upset when he heard 'bout it. Asked me to go with him and some friends to visit the boy tomorrow night and teach him about how things work down here in the Delta."

"Don't do it, R.C." I felt dizzy, scared like something terrible was going to happen. "I swear if you do anything, I'll—"

"Look at you!" R.C. laughed. "Don't get yourself all

worked up for nothin', Mr. Sisbaby. I ain't stupid enough to come and tell you of all people right before I go and do somethin' illegal. It's gonna be talk, nothing else. I'm just doing my citizen's duty to guarantee that white women are safe in our community."

"I'll call Sheriff Smith. I mean it."

"Go ahead." R.C. shrugged. "Nothing to tell. We're just gonna talk to the boy." He patted me on the head. "Night night, Hiram boy. Hope you don't have no bad dreams." R.C. walked across the yard and out through the bushes.

When I came back into the living room, Grampa was asleep in his chair, *The Greenwood Commonwealth* folded in his lap. I wanted to ask him if he'd heard about the trouble in Money and to tell him what R.C. had said. I wanted to ask him what I should do. I almost woke him, but then I decided that I was sixteen years old and could make up my own mind. I went into the kitchen and called the sheriff's office. My hand shook a little as I dialed the phone.

Sheriff Smith wasn't there, so I ended up talking to one of his deputies. I told him everything R.C. had said.

"Ain't nothing to worry 'bout, son," he replied. "R. C. Rydell's sure enough a troublemaker, but that's all he is. I don't expect that he'll even make it to Money; he's too busy getting into mischief down here in his hometown to head up there."

"But he said he was going up there with some men because of that trouble at Bryant's on Wednesday."

"Know all about that. Coloreds round here been talking

about it since yesterday: The word is that some nigra boy from Chicago made ugly remarks and then whistled at Miz Bryant." The deputy chuckled. "Fool boy forgot where he was and what he was, and it's a fact somebody's sure to give that boy a talking to. It'll do him good to learn how things work here in the Delta."

A Negro from Chicago? Emmett! My heart thumped like it was going to rip right out of my chest. "You don't understand. R.C. doesn't just talk. He's dangerous."

"Oh, he likes to think he's dangerous, but I've known him since he was a kid. Ain't gonna be no harm done, believe me."

"But I know R.C. and what he can do. Can't you at least go talk to him? Or maybe pick him up tonight to keep him out of trouble? What if you send somebody by that boy's house, you know, to warn him or to send him back to Chicago right away?"

The deputy sighed. "Lookit, son, we can't be running all round the county for no good reason. Why don't you just let us worry about the law around here? There ain't gonna be no serious trouble; I can guarantee it. Now I gotta get back to work." The phone line clicked and the dial tone sounded like an alarm in my ear.

CHAPTER 10

When I finally fell asleep Friday night, I dreamed that Dad and I were fishing somewhere on a gorgeous morning. The sun filtered through the trees and light reflected off the river like shiny scales, while we sat on the banks enjoying the peace and beauty of the place. Dad looked content and happy, not just with life but with me. We weren't talking, but I could *feel* his love and acceptance. More than anything, more than even my next breath, I wanted to stay there at his side, to bask in the warmth of the morning sun and the security of his affection. He put an arm around my shoulders. It felt warm and strong. And real. I felt the weight of his arm and the movement of his ribs as he breathed. I'd never been closer to him.

Then, for some reason, I stood up and left. I walked up a path away from the river to get something, something that seemed important to me at the time, something I thought would please him.

When I got back, Dad was gone. At first I didn't panic. I sat down exactly where we had been before and waited. I knew he'd return, and when he did, so would all the comfortable, good feelings.

Minutes passed.

Dad didn't come back.

As I sat alone on the bank of that river, the secure, loved feeling I had savored with Dad bled out of me, and a horrible emptiness replaced it. My heart ached for that feeling to return, but it didn't. I knew that moment with Dad was lost forever, and I sat on the riverbank crying for my father.

And for me.

When I woke up, the ache in my chest lingered, and I felt lonelier and sadder than I had ever felt in my life.

All day Saturday, I kept worrying about Emmett. If I thought I could have found his uncle's home, I would've driven out to warn him. I knew they wouldn't have a telephone in a sharecropper's shack, so trying to call him wouldn't have done any good. I felt lousy and helpless, and I said something to Ruthanne about it while she was cleaning up after breakfast.

She shook her head and frowned. "I already heard plenty about his stupid stunt at that white man's store up in Money, and soon as I see him, I'm going to give that boy a talking to he won't forget. It's thoughtful for you to be worrying about him, Hiram, but I'm sure Uncle Mose knows all about what happened and'll keep an eye on Bobo till they get him safe on that train back to Chicago."

Later Grampa could tell I was worried about something, and he did his best to cheer me up, even took me fishing on the Tallahatchie, but that only made me feel worse. It reminded me of all the crap R.C. had done. I went only because I hoped I'd see Emmett so I could warn him and tell him I was sorry I'd let R.C. hurt him, but our fishing trip didn't last long because Grampa tired out so fast, and we left the river without any fish—and without seeing Emmett.

On the way home Grampa said, "You're still looking glummer than a lost puppy, son. Tell you what. We'll have dinner tonight at the Crystal Grill to cheer us up. No better place in the Delta for a good meal and good company."

That night when we got to his favorite restaurant, Grampa really perked up. Everybody in the place knew him. Some people patted him on the back as they passed our table; others stopped to chat, usually about his work on the Council and how they appreciated all he was doing to "save the South." I hadn't seen him enjoy himself that much the whole time I'd been back in Greenwood.

When we got home, Grampa settled into his living room chair to read the *Commonwealth* while I fiddled with the radio looking for a baseball game. I found a Dodgers game and lay on the floor listening to it until I dozed off. Some time later a knock on the door woke me up. Most of the lights in the house were off—it had to be pretty late—and Grampa had already answered the door.

"Evenin', Mr. Hillburn," said one man. "Sorry to be callin' on you so late."

"Yessir, it is late," said another man, "but we gotta talk."

Grampa looked back into the living room and saw I was awake. "Council business, Hiram. Why don't you go on up to bed?" Then, instead of inviting the men into the living room like he did with his regular Council buddies, he stepped outside and talked to them on the porch—with the front light off—before coming back in to tell me he was off to another meeting. "Don't wait up, son," he said. "This looks like it might take all night." I watched him get into the backseat of their car and drive off and then I went upstairs to bed. He must have got back pretty late, because it took me a long time to fall asleep, and I never did hear him come in.

The next day, Sunday, Grampa and I both woke up feeling tired and lazy. The August heat and his diabetes had been wearing on him, and I was haunted by my worries about what R.C. might have done to Emmett the previous night.

I made us a late breakfast, and we spent the rest of the day napping, playing cards, or listening to the radio in the living room. Seemed like neither one of us ever really got awake that day. I thought about asking Grampa if I could use the phone to call long distance to talk to Mom and Dad, but I didn't know what I'd say to them if I did. I had a feeling that maybe Dad would call me, so I didn't mind hanging around the house all day waiting for the phone to ring.

It never did.

Grampa felt better Monday morning, so after breakfast we drove out to the fields. "Little fresh air is what we both need, son," he said. "Sitting around the house all day yesterday didn't do either one of us a bit of good."

As we drove to the fields north of town, I wondered if I should tell Grampa about my fears that R.C. might have done something bad to Emmett, but he seemed so happy to be outside and to see that his crops were about ready to harvest, that I didn't want to ruin his mood.

"Tell you what, Hiram," Grampa said as we pulled away from the fields, "let's drive over to Indianola for lunch. There's a great little café downtown where we can get some catfish that's almost as good as Gramma used to cook." He leaned back into the truck seat and swung his arm out the window and pointed forward. "Drive on, boy. We're having us a day trip."

"Grampa," I said as we headed up the highway, "did you and Dad ever fish together much, you know, when he was little?"

"Your daddy used to love fishing," Grampa said. "He'd badger me all week to take him fishing on Saturday morning. He didn't mind getting up early. Didn't mind sitting still on the riverbank. Didn't mind spending the whole damn day in the same spot holding a fishing rod."

I could hardly believe what I'd just heard: Dad fishing? He'd never said a word about it. We didn't even own any poles. "So when did he change? I mean, he's never taken me fishing."

"When your daddy got to be older, everything went crazy. He didn't want to go fishing, didn't want to have anything to do with me, and I don't mind telling you that his attitude rubbed me the wrong way. This was my only child; all my life I'd planned that we'd spend time together, fishing, working out in the fields, and when he didn't want to do that anymore, I started pushing him. Making him go. Making him do what I wanted him to do." He shook his head. "And that didn't do a damn bit of good except to push him away from me and my life. Don't get me wrong, son, your daddy never gave us a lick of trouble. He got good grades, behaved himself in school, did everything right, but he wasn't doing it my way, and I let him know it. By the time he was in high school, we hardly talked anymore." He sighed. "And you yourself know that things haven't changed much since then. Maybe they've even gotten worse."

"That's kind of what worries me," I said. "The same stuff is happening with me and Dad. Before I came down here, I didn't care about how we got along—and I didn't care because I thought *he* didn't care, but I don't like how things are with me and Dad, and now I'm starting to think that maybe he doesn't either. The problem is, I don't know what to do about it."

"It can't be one way, I know that," said Grampa. "To get connected, you've both got to reach out, you've both got to be willing to give a little. My problem always was I wouldn't give an inch."

"Maybe Dad and I are too much like that; neither one of us is willing to make an effort to understand the other."

"I'll tell you, son, that's one family trait I wish hadn't been passed on. There's lots in you that you, your daddy, or I can't do a thing about, but this is something you can change. And believe me, a good relationship between a father and his son is worth it. It's worth more than you can know."

"Grampa, sometimes I wish that Dad and me could be like you and me."

Grampa looked sad when he heard that, and he said quietly, "So do I, son. So do I."

When we got back home, there was a note on the door from Ruthanne. It was written in her perfect looping cursive handwriting and in the careful English she always used when she wrote something.

"Dear Mr. Earl," it read, "I am truly sorry I cannot be at work today. My extended family has experienced a tragedy, and I must attend to their immediate needs. I shall do my utmost to be at work on time tomorrow morning. Please excuse my unavoidable absence.

"Very sincerely yours, Ruthanne Parker."

"Good thing we had that big catfish lunch in Indianola today," Grampa said as he handed me the note and opened the front door. "Grab the newspaper there, Hiram, and let's get inside and figure out what we can do to keep from starving until we see Ruthanne again."

I picked up the *Commonwealth* off the porch and followed Grampa into the house. When he got settled into his favorite chair, I handed him the paper and headed for the kitchen to put something together for dinner. "Scrambled eggs and toast okay?" I asked.

"Throw in a little onion if you can find it," he called over his shoulder as he snapped open the evening paper. "Looks like we're going to survive after all."

I had just set the frying pan on the stove when Grampa called for me. I switched off the burner and trotted back into the living room. "Grampa, are you all right?"

"Take a look at this," he said, handing me the paper. His face had turned serious and pale.

Splashed across the front page was the headline: "Chicago Negro Youth Abducted by Three White Men at Money."

I felt like I'd been kicked in the stomach. I skimmed the article: Emmett had been missing since early Sunday morning. Three white men and a woman had gone to his uncle's home and asked if the boy from Chicago was there. They took Emmett out to their car where a white woman identified him as the one who had made "ugly remarks" to her, and then put him in the car and drove off. No one had seen Emmett since. The sheriff had already arrested Roy Bryant and J. W. Milam for the kidnapping—even though they claimed they had released Emmett—and was searching for a third man.

"I can't believe this! I called the sheriff's office. I told them about R.C. I warned them that something like . . ." My voice choked up and I had to sit down. "It's R.C. They've got to know that. I told them Friday night."

"What are you talking about?" Grampa looked worried.

"The third man! R. C. Rydell told me he was going to make trouble."

"Now don't go jumping to conclusions, son," said Grampa.

"Just because R.C. was talking big Friday doesn't mean he had something to do with this."

"But he told me he was going up to Money with some other men. He said they were just going to do some talking, but I knew it wouldn't stop at that. I knew something bad was going to happen. I should've done more. I could've stopped R.C. I could've found Emmett and warned him." My whole body felt cold and hard, like a rock sinking to the bottom of a lake.

Grampa was about to say something when the phone rang. I went into the kitchen and answered it.

"This is Sheriff George Smith, and I'm wondering if I could speak to Hiram Hillburn."

"Yessir," I said. "That's me." I gulped. What had R.C. told the sheriff? Had he blamed me for what had happened?

"My deputy said you called here Friday night with some information about R. C. Rydell and his plans to call on a Negro boy Saturday night."

"Yessir."

"You seen R.C. lately?"

"Not since that night."

"He say anything to you about what he planned on doing?"

I took a deep breath. "He said he was going up to Money with a couple other men to talk to a Negro boy about the trouble at the Bryant store. I tried to stop him. I didn't want anything to happen. I called your office and told—"

"Hold on, boy. You did just fine. Now, you got any idea

where R.C. might be? He didn't say anything about where he might be heading, did he?"

"Last I knew he was headed home."

Sheriff Smith cleared his throat. "I thank you, Hiram, for your help in this case. One more question: How long are you planning on staying in Greenwood?"

"I got a ticket for Wednesday's train. My dad wants me back in time for school."

"Well, you'd better call your daddy and tell him you're not going to be able to make that train. I'm afraid we might be needing you around here for the next little while."

CHAPTER 11

Grampa didn't seem too worried about the sheriff's phone call. "George Smith is all right," he said. "He's just doing his job. My guess is that when he finally catches up with R. C. Rydell, he's going to want you around to back up your story. You'll be fine, Hiram, I promise. And look on the bright side: We'll get to have a little more time together."

We talked for a few minutes, then Grampa went to the kitchen to use the phone. He dialed the operator and asked her to connect him with my parents' phone number. While I stood behind him waiting for the call to be put through, I wondered how Mom and Dad would take it. Would Dad even believe Grampa, or would he think it was some kind of trick to keep me in Greenwood longer? I still felt cold and nervous. The thought of being the guy who got R. C. Rydell in big trouble with the police made me want to get out of Greenwood while I was still breathing.

"Hello, Dee?" Grampa said into the phone. "This is Earl. . . . Yes, calling long distance. . . . No, Hiram is fine, but there is some complication just now. Is Harlan home? . . . I see. Well, there's been some mischief down here, none of it Hiram's doing, of course, but the sheriff is in the middle of tracking down some of the troublemakers, and he might need Hiram here to confirm a detail or two. . . . No, no, it's nothing serious at all, just a hotheaded kid acting stupid. Of course, Hiram is welcome to stay here, you know that. I'll take good care of him until this whole thing is over, then I'll make sure he gets on the next train for Arizona. . . . Yes. . . . Yes, dear, I will."

Grampa handed me the phone. "She wants to talk to you."

"Hiram?" Mom sounded worried. "You're not in trouble, are you?"

"It's like Grampa said. The sheriff just wants me to stick around in case I have to answer questions or something. I'll be all right."

"Your father's not going to be pleased when he hears about this. You know how he feels about Greenwood."

"Well, tell him that being here has helped me appreciate what he's been saying all along. I still love it here and love being with Grampa, but I think maybe I understand Dad a little better now. At least I hope I do."

"Do you need me or Dad to come out there? One of us could be in Greenwood in a few days."

"I'll be fine with Grampa, and I'll come home as soon as I can. Everything'll be okay." I tried to say that like I believed it.

"Just you remember who you are, Hiram Hillburn, and be sure you do what is right no matter what. And help your grampa as much as you can. You're not there on vacation anymore."

"Thanks, Mom."

"I love you, son."

"Love you too," I said before I hung up.

Later that night Grampa talked to Sheriff Smith on the phone just to make sure he understood everything that was going on. He told me about the call before we went to bed.

"George thinks this might go to trial, and if it does, and if it turns out R.C. was involved with those peckerwoods, he'll need you to testify. He's got other evidence, of course, but your story will help place R.C. in the picture. I told him I didn't think involving you in this whole mess was necessary, but he insisted on keeping you around. I tell you one thing, Hiram, if R. C. Rydell is involved in this, he's in deep trouble. This isn't bullying. They're after him for kidnapping. George thinks R.C. might be holding that Negro boy somewhere right now. There's no telling what he might have done."

That's exactly what I was afraid of.

Ruthanne showed up to work the next morning looking exhausted. She'd been out to Emmett's uncle's home trying to offer what help she could. "Uncle Mose is sick with worry," she said. "Those white men came into their home in the middle of the night with a flashlight and a gun and demanded to see Bobo. Uncle Mose begged them to leave him there; he promised he'd give Bobo a good licking himself, but they wouldn't listen." Her eyes glistened with tears. "They made the boy get dressed and dragged him out to their car, and nobody's seen or heard from him since." Ruthanne held back a sob, but her voice quivered when she said, "That poor boy and his mama. This is plain awful."

The next evening's paper had little to say about the kidnapping. "Negro Youth Still Missing," read the front-page headline. The short article summarized the details in the case, including that the police were still looking for a third man and that they were conducting intense searches for Emmett up around Money.

I wondered if they'd find R.C.

I wondered if they'd find Emmett.

Wednesday evening's paper answered one of my questions: They found Emmett.

MISSING CHICAGO NEGRO YOUTH FOUND IN TALLAHATCHIE RIVER

August 31, 1955

The body of a 14-year-old kidnapped Chicago Negro boy was found floating in the Tallahatchie River this morning. Discovery of the body was made by a young fisherman named Mims, who was inspecting his trot line. The body was in shallow water near the bank, it was reported, and was found at Pecan Point near Phillipp.

Young Mims notified Sheriff H. C. Strider at Charleston in Tallahatchie County of his find. He immediately called the sheriff's office in Greenwood and reported the matter.

Deputy Sheriff John Edd Cothran and Deputy Sheriff Ed Weber went to the scene and carried Mose Wright, uncle of the youth, along in order to make identification of the body. It was brought back to Greenwood and turned over to the Century Burial Association, local Negro undertakers.

Officers said that the body had been weighed down with a cotton gin pulley tied with barbed wire. There was also a bullet hole in his head.

Three white men and a woman took the boy from his uncle's home early Sunday after the boy allegedly made "ugly remarks" to a white woman.

Two white men, Roy Bryant and his half brother J. W. Milam, have been charged with kidnapping. The sheriff's office said that an additional charge of murder will be made since the turn of events.

Sheriff George W. Smith said several days ago after the happening that he was afraid of foul play.

Young Till allegedly made the ugly remarks to Mrs. Bryant, wife of the storekeeper who faces a kidnapping charge. The youth was visiting his uncle, Mose Wright, a tenant farmer.

Sheriff Smith said Bryant admitted taking the boy from his uncle's home but said the youth was released when Mrs. Bryant said he was not the boy who made the remarks to her.

Sheriff Smith said the investigation showed:

Young Till and several other Negro youths went to the Bryant store in the Money community and Till went in and allegedly made the remarks.

Early Sunday, a car carrying three men and a woman drove up to Wright's house. One of the men asked Wright if the boy from Chicago was there. Two men brought the boy out of the house.

Wright asked where they were taking his nephew. One of the men replied, "Nowhere if he's not the right one."

When I put the newspaper down, my hands were shaky and cold. Emmett was dead, murdered. The article said nothing about R. C. Rydell, but I figured the sheriff must still be looking for him. Was R.C. involved in the murder? I knew he was, and I hoped the police would find him—soon.

And what about Naomi? If R.C. skipped town or ended up in jail, she'd be left alone with her dad. I didn't even want to think how much more miserable her life might become in that shack down along the Yazoo.

Grampa interrupted my thoughts when he whistled softly after reading the article. "I can't believe they killed that boy." He rubbed his hand across his face and muttered to himself, "There's going to be hell to pay now." He still looked pale as he folded the paper on his lap, creased it carefully in half, and set it on the table next to his chair. "Hiram, those boys went too far, way too far. For his sake, I sure hope your friend wasn't involved in this mess. I never did think much of R. C. Rydell, but I never took him for a murderer."

"R.C.'s not my friend, Grampa," I reminded him without looking at him. "I told you how he acted."

"Of course he's not your friend. A Hillburn usually has better sense than getting mixed up with people like these." Grampa rapped his knuckles on the folded newspaper. "People all over the United States are hearing about what's happened down here and wondering what kind of uncivilized brutes live in Mississippi. Those peckerwoods who did this are a shame to all of us in the Delta. No self-respecting Southern gentleman would lower himself to go this far."

Grampa's reaction bothered me. He seemed more concerned about the negative press than about what had happened to Emmett Till.

He kept on complaining. "The radio said that colored boy's mama up in Chicago is blaming everyone in Mississippi for what's happened, said she said, 'The entire state of Mississippi is going to pay for this.' The woman's grief is understandable, Hiram, but she's got no cause to blame all of us for what a couple redneck peckerwoods did in the middle of the night.

"Before we know it, the NAACP and all those bleeding-heart Northerners are going to use this as another excuse for integration. They're going to come down here and cry about how we treat our Negroes and how we've got to mix the races in our schools. That's what really makes me mad, son: Those ignorant boys have stirred up a hornet's nest of trouble."

"But what about Emmett?" I asked. "They killed him. Doesn't that make you mad?"

"Of course those boys went too far. Whatever that colored boy deserved, he didn't deserve getting shot and tossed into the Tallahatchie, that's for sure."

I wanted to yell at Grampa. A boy was murdered just for acting cocky! I wanted to say something, something mean and hard that would knock some sense into him, but I knew nothing I could say would change him, and I had a glimpse into why Dad and Grampa never got along.

"Mr. Hiram," called Ruthanne from the front door, "you got a visitor." I left Grampa sulking in his chair and went to the front porch where Ruthanne stood talking to Naomi. Naomi had her head down, as she always did when she spoke to adults. "Miz Ruthanne," she said, "I just want you to know how awful sorry I am for what's happened to your cousin's nephew. It's an evil thing, a terrible hateful thing." A tear rolled down her cheek and Ruthanne hugged her.

"Now thank you, honey," said Ruthanne. "Lord knows it surely does help to share grief with somebody else." She sighed and let go of Naomi. "Child, I do appreciate your sympathy, but you didn't come here just to talk to me. I'm heading on home anyway, so you and Mr. Hiram can set out here and talk if you like."

Naomi nodded and sat in the porch swing while Ruthanne stood there looking washed out and exhausted. I remembered how I had felt when Gramma died and wondered how Ruthanne was feeling. Emmett's death had been a surprise, just like Gramma's had been, but his was a brutal murder, not a quiet slipping away in the middle of the night.

"Ruthanne," I said, "I feel terrible about Emmett. I don't know what I can do or say. I wish I could have . . . I'll remember him and his family in my prayers."

"Thank you, Hiram. We'll all be praying too, praying for the good Lord's mercy. Good night, you two," she said and went down the front steps.

When she had gone, I sat next to Naomi.

"I can't believe it, Hiram," she whispered. "They *killed* that boy. When I think about how he must have felt, what he must've been thinking those last hours . . . how *afraid* he woulda been." She shivered. "Why do men do things like that? Why do they have to hurt people?"

I had no answer, so we sat without talking as our swing rocked gently in the late August breeze. Even though the horrible things that had been done to Emmett filled my head, it was comforting to be with Naomi. Like Ruthanne said, it helps to have someone to share grief with.

After a few minutes, Naomi leaned her head on my shoulder and said, "I feel awful. And I'm just so scared."

For the next two days Greenwood hummed with talk about Emmett Till. Some wondered who the third man might be. Others hoped Bryant and Milam got the full punishment of the law. A few thought Bryant and Milam had done nothing wrong. "Nigger boy shoulda knowed better," I overheard someone say at the River Café. "I'm mighty glad we still got men in the Delta who won't put up with uppity niggers from the North. Maybe that message'll get around."

That night, Grampa pointed to a front page article he had just read in the *Commonwealth*. "They got that right," he said. "Got it dead right. Listen to this, Hiram."

Grampa read the article aloud, sounding as dramatic as a radio announcer:

A Just Appraisal
(An Editorial)

September 2, 1955

The State of Mississippi, and Leflore and Talla-hatchie counties in particular, have been brought into the focus of national attention within the past few days as a result of the brutal murder of Emmett Louis Till, a 14-year-old Chicago Negro boy. This deplorable incident has made our section the target of unjustifiable criticism, thoughtless accusations, and avenging threats.

We can understand the heartbreak of the mother of the dead boy and we offer our sympathy and express our deep regret that this terrible thing has happened to her, but her determination to see that "Mississippi is going to pay for this," charging the entire state with the guilt of those who took the law into their own hands, is evidence of the poison selfish men have planted in the minds of people outside the South. If the mother had expressed the determination to see that the guilty parties "must pay for this crime," she would have expressed the sincere desires of the people of Mississippi.

The NAACP has only revealed again its blindness and injustice in charging that "Mississippi has decided to maintain white supremacy by murdering children," and that "the killers of the boy felt free to lynch him because there is in the entire state no restraining influence, not in the state capital, among the daily newspapers, the clergy, nor any segment of the so-called better citizens." From its headquarters in New York it has charged every citizen of the state with being an accomplice in the crime. On the basis of one murder it has judged the character, honor, and integrity of the entire population. One wonders why it did not judge the people of our state by the incident of a few months ago when a ten-year-old white girl in the same community risked her life in the same river, only a few miles from where the body of the fourteen-year-old boy was found, to save the life of a Negro woman who was drowning.

The citizens of this area are determined that the guilty parties shall be punished to the full extent of the law and that justice shall be administered irrespective of the color of the victim or the criminals. The greatest enemies of this justice are the outside groups and individuals who chill the flames of indignation aroused by such crimes by wholesale and indiscriminate accusations against the law-abiding and justice-loving people of our state. If the NAACP and other groups want justice, then let them cease throwing stones at the prosecution, judge, and jury. If they're as concerned about this matter as they claim, then let them judge the evidence in the case and cease using the case as manufactured evidence to wage war against segregation.

The people of Mississippi are no more responsible for this tragic murder and no more condone it than the people of New York, or any other state, are responsible for and condone murders committed there, but every decent and respectable citizen of this state will assume his or her responsibility for seeing that justice is administered through the courts of law and that guilty parties shall pay for their crime.

He set the paper down. "See here? We can't be blamed for the sorry actions of a couple local hotheads who haven't got an ounce of common sense between them. Those boys being from Mississippi shouldn't condemn the whole lot of us. Just because we believe in segregation, in the inequality of the races, or just because we might even know a couple dumb peckerwoods from the next county doesn't make us evil. *Those* boys did the killing, not me, you, or the entire state of Mississippi."

He shifted in his chair, looking like he'd made up his mind about something. "No blame here, no sir, and I don't care what that boy's mama or the NAACP say about it."

"But what about R.C., Grampa? The paper's been saying that there was a third man involved in it."

"The law'll take care of him. Sooner or later R. C. Rydell's going to end up in a bad way, Hiram. If he doesn't get hung for this, it'll be something else down the road. The boy's got bad blood and that's all there is to it. And, Hiram, I've been thinking about this, and it seems to me there's no need for you getting mixed up in this mess. R.C. has dug his own grave. My guess is that once the sheriff catches up with him, things'll be plain as day and you won't need to say anything about anybody. You'll be on your way back to Arizona before you know it."

I hoped Grampa was right, but I knew that if I did have to say anything to Sheriff Smith about R.C., I'd be lucky to get out of Greenwood alive.

CHAPTER 12

Most of the next day I fretted about what to do. Had R.C. heard that I'd talked to the sheriff? Was he looking for me? If he was, would he come at night, catch me in the backyard when I wasn't expecting him? Would he pull me into an alley when I was downtown? Would he be hiding out near one of my fishing holes, waiting to ambush me? Or would he be crazy and cocky enough just to walk up to the front door and knock?

When we were kids, I figured R.C. was plain mean, but after what happened to Emmett, I knew R.C. was worse than mean. For the first time in my life, I worried about dying, not just the death part, but the messy and painful things that would lead up to the dying, the kinds of things that would make a guy welcome death. I wanted to forget the sheriff's orders, pack up my things, and jump on the next train out of Greenwood.

Early that evening while Grampa was dozing in his chair and I was flipping through old magazines trying to keep my mind off the trial, torture, death, and R. C. Rydell, a loud knock on the front door just about pushed my heart right through my chest.

I didn't move. Grampa's snoring paused a moment, but he didn't wake up.

The pounding again.

"Grampa?" I whispered. "Grampa, somebody's at the door."

He was dead asleep.

More pounding.

R.C.? My mind raced to figure out what to do. Grampa's pickup sat in the driveway, so it was obvious we were home. I could wake Grampa, but he'd be no good against R.C., and if he got in the way, R.C. probably would hurt him too. I could sneak out the back, but that'd mean leaving Grampa alone.

Believe me, I'm no hero, but right then I realized that as long as I was in Greenwood, R.C. could get me if he wanted to, and I'd have to face up to him sooner or later. I took another look at Grampa—asleep. "I'll get it," I said, even though he couldn't hear me.

It was still summer, but my hand felt ice cold as I gripped the knob to open the door; it was like opening my own coffin. I took a deep breath, turned the handle, and braced myself for a fist smashing my front teeth.

Where I had expected to see R. C. Rydell ready to rip my head off stood a uniformed deputy. He had a clipboard and some papers in his hand.

"You Hiram Hillburn?"

Slumping against the doorway, I tipped my head back and let out a sigh.

"Lookit here, boy," the deputy snapped. "You Hiram Hillburn or not?"

I stepped through the front door and pulled it closed behind me. "Yessir." My voice shook a little.

"Consider yourself served, son." He handed me a sealed envelope, then held out his clipboard. "Sign here, and that lets the judge know you received this subpoena to appear in court."

"Court?"

"Don't tell me Sheriff Smith never said nothing to you about the trial they're fixing to have up in Sumner? You know, 'bout that colored boy that got himself kidnapped and killed?"

"He asked me to stay in Greenwood, but he didn't say anything about a trial."

The deputy handed me a pencil and tapped the clipboard. "Not my problem, son. Signing this only means I handed you the subpoena; whether or not you end up testifying in court is up to the judge and the lawyers. And I suppose, maybe because you're a juvenile, you won't even have to testify if you don't want to. But I'm just delivering this"—he paused, looking at the clipboard—"and if you'll sign it, I can get back to work."

I signed the form and he left.

Grampa was awake when I came back into the house. "Naomi again?"

"Nosir, it was a deputy. He brought me this." I handed the envelope to Grampa; he opened it and read the subpoena. When he finished, he didn't say anything for a while.

Finally, he said, "I don't like this, son, not one bit. It's one thing for you to talk to George Smith about what R.C.'s done and said, but testifying in court . . . you're just a boy, and this business is too dirty for you to be getting mixed up in."

"Do I have a choice?"

"Of course you have a choice. Last I checked, we're still living in the United States of America, regardless of what the NAACP and those outside agitators say. If I was you, Hiram, I'd keep my mouth shut about this whole thing. It's going to be ugly, maybe even dangerous. Northern rabble-rousers will be there, and some of our local rednecks aren't going to take too kindly to that. And didn't you say that R.C. had threatened you?"

"Not exactly threatened, but I sure felt warned; he doesn't want me talking to Sheriff Smith about what he did to Emmett while we were fishing."

"That boy's dangerous. You ought to lay low, keep quiet, and let things work themselves out; no need for you to risk getting hurt. The judge can make you appear in court, but you don't have to tell everything you know, especially when testifying might put you in serious danger."

I nodded. R.C. scared me, for sure, but shouldn't I tell all the truth, even if I was afraid?

"Now, what about this R. C. Rydell?" Grampa asked. "You

want me to talk to the sheriff about his threatening you? You got a right to feel safe here, anywhere, and the law's bound to protect you. If you're worried that he's going to come after you, I can ask the sheriff to have him locked up if they find him, or maybe have a deputy keep an eye on the house while you're here. You know that boy, Hiram; you know he can be real trouble."

"I guess I wouldn't mind if a deputy kind of hung around here for a while, just in case." I hoped I'd never see R.C. again, because if he really wanted to get me, having a deputy around wasn't going to stop him.

"If you talk in court, Hiram, you're going to stir up R.C. pretty good. There's no way you can keep it secret. Trials are public, and whatever gets said is going to show up in the *Commonwealth*, so even if old R.C. has enough sense to steer clear of the Sumner courthouse, he's going to hear that you spoke against him in court."

Thinking about R.C made me shiver. "I know I'd be crazy to tell everything at that trial; R.C. scares me to death. If I had my choice, I'd be on a train tonight headed back to Tempe. But Emmett Till is dead, Grampa, for no good reason. He had as much right to be here in Leflore County as I do. He was just a kid, a kid like me—"

"Hold on, son. He was a colored boy who didn't know his place."

"That doesn't give R.C. and those two other men the right to *murder* him."

Grampa's face turned serious. "You don't know for sure

who did the killing, Hiram, and you've got to remember that Chicago boy made his own trouble. If he'd stayed in his place, he'd be alive today, and believe me, son, I truly wish none of this had happened." Grampa looked exhausted. "Not a single bit of it."

"But it did happen, and that boy is dead, and we both know that R. C. Rydell had something to do with it. Sure he scares me, but don't I owe Emmett something? Isn't it my duty to do something about it?"

"You don't owe that boy a damn thing. For starters, he's dead. All the talking in the world isn't going to change that. And you're in the Delta, son. No jury down here would even dream of punishing white boys for putting a Negro in his place. Sure, they got carried away something awful, but they're local men, *white* men. The only thing you'll do by speaking up in that trial is to get yourself hurt, maybe hurt bad."

Grampa sounded so wrongheaded, I couldn't believe it. Maybe some of what Dad was always spouting about equality and the American dream had rubbed off on me. "Don't American laws apply in the Delta? What R.C. and those two men did was wrong, Grampa. It makes me sick just to think about it."

"Because you're a decent young man. You come from good stock, Hiram."

"If I'm so decent, shouldn't I tell what I know about R.C.? He *killed* a boy, Grampa, and I could've stopped him."

"Now, Hiram, you already did more than you had to, calling the sheriff and everything. Not many boys your age would've had the courage to—"

"But I *should* have done more. Maybe I could have stopped R.C. that night, made him stay here. Maybe if I had followed him . . ."

Grampa waved his hand impatiently. "You're forgetting that two grown men are already in jail for the crime, and they've admitted to kidnapping the boy. They would have done what they did whether or not R.C. was there—and you don't know for sure that he was there, Hiram."

"But he told me he was going to Money with a couple of men and that they were going to teach a Northern Negro a lesson. Emmett disappeared the next night."

"Just because he planned to go up there doesn't mean he ever did. Look at what you're saying, son. You've already convicted R.C. for a crime you can't be sure he committed. How are you going to look in court? Are you willing to accuse a boy everybody knows is a big talker of kidnapping *and* murder based on a conversation you had with him one night?"

"Grampa, I *know* R.C. and what he can do. I've seen what he's done before."

"So what? Do you have proof that he went to Mose Wright's house that night? That he was with Bryant and Milam? That he helped them kill that boy? You got any proof of that?"

"But he said—"

"Don't matter what he *said*, Hiram, the court's interested

in what he did, in what can be *proven* beyond a reasonable doubt. Do you really think that a jury made up of white Delta men is going to take your word over that of a local boy? Like I said, if you tell everything in that trial, the only thing you're going to do is get yourself hurt and embarrass me."

"*Embarrass* you?"

"People around here have long memories, son. They remember how your daddy was, how I couldn't talk or whip any sense into him when he got to be your age. You have no idea how humiliating it is when a boy shames his family! Friends and neighbors said they understood, that they felt sorry about how Harlan and I battled, but I know that behind my back they talked about how I was a poor father, that if I had raised Harlan right, he wouldn't have shamed me." His voice trailed off. "Your daddy . . . you can't be like your daddy."

Grampa sat quietly until Ruthanne called us to supper. He looked up, a little confused, like he'd been dreaming or something, and waved me over to help him out of his chair.

"You get in court and talk against white folks, Hiram, and people around here'll see your daddy in you. Contrary, that's what he was. Didn't like the South, the Southern ways. The Delta wasn't good enough for him." He wiped his mouth, and his hand trembled. "I don't think I could take it again. That public condemnation. Friends gossiping. Feeling shame because of what my boy did and said. I raised you different, Hiram. You are not like your father. You're a

Delta boy, through and through." Grampa patted my arm. "You're a good boy, son, and I've been proud of you. I know you'll do the right thing."

Neither one of us said much during supper. Grampa seemed worn out, tired, and like his mind was on something else, and I just didn't feel like talking. Ruthanne had made one of my favorite dinners, but it didn't taste very good that night. Thinking about R.C., Emmett, Dad and Grampa, and the trial pretty much ruined me for eating. I managed a drumstick and a couple scoops of mashed potatoes and coleslaw and then excused myself. I needed to get out of the house. I needed to see Naomi.

Grampa said nothing when I left the table and headed for the kitchen.

"You feeling all right, Mr. Hiram?" asked Ruthanne when I came in. "Not like you to leave my fried chicken and fixings uneaten like that."

I shrugged. "Just been worrying about this trial."

"You let the judge and lawyers worry about that. And I bet they're plenty worried themselves. I never thought I'd see it happen, but they got two white men sitting in jail right now, and they're going to send 'em to trial. Far as I know, this is the first time in the history of Mississippi that white men are gonna be made to account for what they done to a black man." Ruthanne's eyes filled with tears. "Nothing any jury can do to bring Emmett back, but they sure can let folks in the Delta know that things are changing. Changing at last."

"I'm really sorry about Emmett, Ruthanne. Awful sorry." I don't know why, but I felt like crying then. I blinked the tears back. "I wish it had never happened. It should've never happened."

"I appreciate that, Mr. Hiram," she said as she dabbed her eyes. "Ain't nothing you could've done about it, I know, but I do appreciate your sympathies."

"But maybe I could have done something. Maybe I can now."

"What's done is done. You couldn't have stopped old Milam and Bryant anyway. The law and the good Lord'll take care of those two and anyone else mixed up in their wickedness."

Somehow I felt mixed up in their wickedness, mixed up and not knowing how to get out of it.

Ruthanne took a deep breath, ready to change the subject. "You heading outside?"

"Thought I'd take a walk; I need to get out of the house for a while."

She pointed to the kitchen garbage pail next to the back door. "Why don't you take that with you to the garbage on your way out? And, Mr. Hiram," Ruthanne said, smiling, "don't you be too late talking with that Naomi girl. You know how her daddy gets."

"I never said anything about Naomi; I just—"

"Don't 'I just' me, Hiram Hillburn. I got boys of my own back home. Now get this trash and yourself out of the house before that poor girl starts worrying about what happened to you."

It felt good to be outside. A few stars had edged over the dark tree-lined horizon. A light breeze stirred the humid night air, and the steady drone of frogs and crickets was the only sound as I emptied the trash into the garbage can behind the garage and walked along the driveway to the sidewalk in front of the house. As I walked through the shadows of the trees that lined the sidewalk, I felt like I was leaving the worries about R.C. and the trial behind.

It didn't take long to get to the bridge, and I felt better than I had all day when I saw Naomi leaning over the bridge railing, looking down into the dark water of the Yazoo. Her hair swayed in the night breeze, hiding her face. She didn't move when I stood alongside her and leaned over the railing myself.

"What're you looking at?" My arm rested next to Naomi's, barely touching.

"The color of the river. During the day it looks so yellow-green, but soon as it's dark, you'd never know it ever had a speck of color in it. Where's all that color go, I wonder."

Without talking, we watched the dark currents of the Yazoo swirl under the bridge below us. Finally, Naomi turned and faced me. "Hey, Hiram."

"Hey, Naomi. You been here long?"

"A while. Tonight wasn't a good night to be home. Pa's on a tear again." She turned around and leaned against the railing. No bruises, at least none I could see. That meant she had gotten out in time.

"Drinking?"

"Always that. But the last couple days the sheriff's come

by looking for R.C., and Pa don't know where he is. Sheriff thinks Pa's lying and warned him that R.C.'s a fugitive, and if Pa's hiding him, he'll land himself in jail. Soon as the sheriff leaves, Pa cusses him, R.C., the NAACP, President Eisenhower, and anybody else he's mad at. Then he starts up drinking again and slows down for a while—and that's when I know I got to get out of there."

"What's the sheriff want R.C. for?" I asked.

"Says he just wants to ask him some questions 'bout that Negro boy got killed up in Money."

"He say why?"

"The way R.C. talks, I s'pose; everybody knows he hates Negroes and how he treats them. He's been in trouble with the law plenty of times before, but this time it galls Pa something awful. He rants and raves: 'Never thought I'd live to see the day when a white lawman would bother a white citizen of the state of Mississippi 'bout nigger trouble. R.C. ain't no saint, not by a long shot, but my boy's white, and the law got no business worrying him 'bout some black boy floated up in the Tallahatchie.' It makes him hateful, Hiram. Worse than drinking."

"You seen R.C. lately?"

"Not since Sunday. I don't know where he is, and I'm worried. I'm sure he knows the sheriff's after him. Ain't the first time he's disappeared for a while."

"Do you think he had anything to do with that trouble in Money?"

"R.C.'s done a lot of stupid things, but he's my brother,

Hiram; I don't think he'd murder somebody." She looked at me, a little unsure of herself.

"I guess they're planning on having a big trial up in Sumner," I said.

Naomi nodded.

"Sheriff wants me to be ready to testify. I got a subpoena today."

"Testify for what? How could you know anything about that murder? You don't even know anybody in Money."

"I know R.C."

"So what? Lots of people know R.C. Why do they want you?"

I told her what R.C. had said the night before the kidnapping. "Next day Emmett Till was missing—and so was R.C."

Naomi's face turned sad. "You think R.C. was with those men?"

"I don't know. That day R.C. and I went fishing, we met Emmett Till and some of his friends at the river. R.C. did something terrible to him."

"Did he hurt him?"

"No, but he scared and shamed him. I don't know, Naomi. If you'd seen how R.C. acted at the river, how cold-blooded he was. Then after he told me he was going to Money—"

"You can't talk about this in court, Hiram." Naomi's eyes opened wide. "You can't say another thing about this."

"I know he's your brother, and it'll be bad for him if anything—"

"Blast my brother. It'll be bad for *you*. Do you think R.C. or any of his peckerwood friends will let you get away with speaking against white men for doing something to a Negro? And even if you get back to Arizona, do you know what they'll do to your grampa? You can't talk in court, Hiram, you just can't. If anything happened to you, if R.C. did something to you"—her voice shook—"I just couldn't stand it!" She grabbed my hand and squeezed it, hard. "You stay away from that trial, Hiram Hillburn. I don't care if you have to sneak out of town and I never see you again, but you stay away from that trial. You just stay away, hear me?" Then she leaned into me and started to cry.

I held her while she buried her face against my chest, and I wanted to stay with her like that for as long as I could. Holding her made me forget about everything else that had gone wrong that Mississippi summer. Right then the only thing I wanted to remember about my weeks in Greenwood was standing alone with Naomi Rydell on the Yazoo bridge thinking not about Emmett, or R.C., or Grampa, or Dad, but about Naomi and how I wanted to protect her.

CHAPTER 13

Naomi wouldn't let me walk her home that night. "Who knows what kind of mood Pa'll be in? And besides, R.C. might be around."

I sure didn't want to run into R.C., but I didn't want Naomi walking home alone either.

"I can get home fine by myself, Hiram," she insisted. "Been doing it for years and haven't had a problem yet."

Before we said good-bye, she took my hand in both of hers and stared at me, her eyes glistening in the dark. "You remember what I told you about that trial. It won't do nobody no good if you get up and talk, so decide right now you'll have nothing to do with it." She squeezed my hand. "Promise, Hiram. Promise you won't go to the trial, won't say anything about R.C. or anything else."

"Maybe they won't even ask me to testify. Maybe I'll go

and just sit around at the trial and the lawyers will decide they don't want to hear from me. There hasn't been anything in the *Commonwealth* about the third man for a while, so maybe they've given up looking for R.C. Or maybe the district attorney decided just to go after Bryant and Milam because they've already confessed to kidnapping."

"And maybe you're wrong. Don't do it, Hiram. Don't be stupid."

Time passed as slow as mud. Mom called every three or four days to see how I was doing. We never talked long, and we never talked about Dad. Except once. "Your father and I want you to know that we're very concerned about your safety, Hiram. Are you *sure* things are going to stay under control?"

"Mom, it's going to be all right. I don't even know for sure if I'll end up talking in the trial anyway."

"Still, we'd feel better if . . ." She paused. "Hiram, your father wants to speak to you."

Dad wanted to talk to me? I couldn't believe it.

"Hiram?"

"Hey, Dad."

He cleared his throat. "Son, I want you to know that your mother or I will be out there immediately if you need us. We've even checked into one of us flying there if we have to. We're worried about this trial mess you've gotten into."

"It's going to be okay. Grampa told me—"

"Your grandfather!" he said quickly and too loud. I heard

him take a breath. "Your grandfather is not in any situation to make promises like that. Besides, *I* am your father, Hiram, and I'm the one who must ultimately be responsible for your safety."

It felt good to hear Dad say that. Very good. "Thanks, Dad, but I've even talked to the sheriff—"

"George Smith?"

"Yessir."

"George is all right. What did he tell you?"

"That there's no way out of the subpoena. I can't leave Greenwood, but he's got someone watching the house, and he promised he'd keep an eye out for anyone who might be looking for trouble. I believe him, Dad. And I'm not scared, honest." *That* was a lie.

"Well, you listen to me. Sheriff Smith is a good man, but you're still in the heart of the Delta, son, and some people down there get crazy about anything they think's going to threaten their Jim Crow ways. Things can get dangerous, fast. You're a smart boy; I expect you to use your head."

"I will. I promise."

"Good. And remember, you need me or your mother, you call us immediately. It'll take some arranging—Mom's got all the kids and I've got school just starting up—but if you need us, one of us will be out there just as fast as we can."

"Grandpa's taking good care of things. I'll be fine, Dad."

"Well, if you're sure, Hiram, but you remember what I said."

I thanked Dad and said good-bye. Nothing he said

changed a thing about what was going on in Greenwood, but almost everything he said made me feel better about him, about *us*.

While I waited for the trial, school had started in Greenwood, and during the day when all the kids in town—including Naomi—were in class, I did what I could to keep from going stir-crazy. Some mornings I'd stay home and read library books or take Grampa's truck and go for a drive in the country. Other times, Grampa and I went out to check his fields. A couple mornings a week we went fishing, but always on the Yazoo instead of the Tallahatchie. It was strange because Grampa never used to fish the Yazoo, but when I asked him about it, he just shrugged it off.

Most afternoons, Grampa dropped in on his friends in the courthouse; like Grampa, they'd all taken a sharp interest in the trial and agreed that they needed to make sure that the NAACP and the outside agitators from the North didn't keep the Mississippi court from doing its job. Most of them worried that the school integration law had started things going in a bad way, and that Northern rabble-rousers would use the trial to force other changes in the South. "We've kept the races separated for a long time and we don't intend to change now," was what Grampa or one of his friends usually ended up saying.

The *Commonwealth* said Sheriff Smith had lots of threatening letters and phone calls from people in Chicago and Mississippi. Somebody even said a caravan of one thousand Negroes was on its way down from Chicago to go after

Milam and Bryant, and that worried the sheriff enough that he called in the National Guard to protect the county jail. On Tuesday, the same day they had a huge funeral for Emmett up in Chicago, the big news around Greenwood, news that surprised most everybody, including Grampa, was that the grand jury had indicted Milam and Bryant for murder and kidnapping. Even though they'd already admitted to kidnapping Emmett Till, they pleaded innocent to both charges.

Because the trial was going to be held up in Tallahatchie County and probably because Sheriff Smith was worrying about keeping the peace, on Wednesday Bryant and Milam got moved to the Tallahatchie County jail up in Charleston. For a while, no one was sure how long they'd be there because no one knew when they'd have the trial—some said it could be all the way in March 1956—but on Friday the *Commonwealth* announced the trial would begin on September 19.

Nine days. Only nine days to decide whether or not I'd tell the truth if I had to sit in the witness chair.

Even if I hadn't been sweating what I'd say if I had to testify, I would have been thinking about the trial most of the time anyway. Almost every day the paper had something about the case, and even if you didn't read the paper, anywhere you went in the county, you'd hear people talking about it. This was the biggest thing ever to hit Greenwood, maybe ever to hit Mississippi.

On a Monday afternoon a week before the trial was supposed to start, Grampa and I were at the courthouse and he was talking with a friend about their White Citizens' Council. I could tell he didn't want me hanging around while they talked, and to be honest, I didn't want to be there either, so I walked down to the lobby to get a Coke from Mr. Paul.

He opened the bottle and set it on the counter. "So, Hiram, you got your wish to stick around in Greenwood a little longer. You been enjoying the extra summer vacation?"

"You know, I used to think I'd love a longer summer vacation, but I'm kind of missing school."

He smiled. "Sometimes when we get what we've always wanted, we realize it's not what we thought it was. When I was your age, I wanted more than anything to get away from Greenwood for a while and find out what the rest of the world was like. Then World War Two came along and gave me my wish. I saw plenty of the world, until this, of course." He pointed to his eyes. "And the whole time I was gone, the only place I could think of was little old Greenwood, Mississippi. Life sure has a funny way of teaching us lessons, don't it?"

"Yessir," I said, "but it seems like some people never learn any of those lessons no matter how many times they're taught."

"Oh, they learn 'em, Hiram, they just don't know it. Sometimes it takes a change of scenery or a good whack in the head to help you recognize the lessons you've learned."

"This change of scenery's sure made me realize that

Greenwood, well, it's different. Lots different from what I thought it was."

"You're not the only person these days wondering about Mississippi. From what I hear, people up north—Negro and white—are pretty hot about that boy's death. For all the trouble this has caused, some folks down here are wishing that boy's body would've stayed at the bottom of the Tallahatchie. And that trial next week's going to heat things up more than anything."

"Do you think the trial will change anything around here?"

"You know anything about the South," Mr. Paul said, "you know we change slower than a tombstone. Oh, it might be a little step forward, but that Negro boy ain't the first to be murdered down here, and I'm afraid he won't be the last."

"Mr. Paul, if you had a chance to be in the trial, you know, like a witness or something, what would you do?"

"If I knew something that proved those two didn't kill that boy, I'd feel obliged to testify, and if I had something that would convict 'em, well, I'd have to plan on closing my shop and heading somewhere far away from Mississippi. But I'd speak up."

"Wouldn't you be scared?"

"You bet I'd be scared. I'd be branded a nigger-lover as soon as I showed up in court, and I suppose I'd be lucky if all I got was a few shot-out windows and a burning cross in my front yard."

"But you'd do it?"

"Other than making the decision harder, being scared wouldn't matter one way or the other." He patted the counter. "You stewing about something serious, Hiram?"

"I guess so. It's just that when things are scary or dangerous, it's hard to see clear what to do."

"Well, the best way to work your way through it is to size up both sides of something, then use all the brains you've got to figure out what's right and what's wrong, and make yourself do the right thing. Do that and no matter what happens, no matter what people say, you'll have no regrets."

That night after dinner I walked over to the bridge, hoping to see Naomi. Nobody was around when I got there, so I stood at our favorite spot and leaned over the railing to watch the Yazoo flow underneath me. Where the bridge lights reflected off the water, I could see the swirls and sticks, clear signs that the current was moving downstream, but where the shadow of the bridge fell, I saw only black, like the river was pouring into a bottomless pit that swallowed up all the water that came its way. I kicked some pebbles between the railing down into the shadows but didn't hear or see any sign that they'd broken the water's surface. The old river kept on moving into the blackness under the bridge, taking with it whatever happened to be along for the ride.

Being with Naomi would've helped, because I had decided that if she asked me again to promise I wouldn't say anything in court, I'd promise. I'd promise her I'd run away from that subpoena and never go near the Sumner courthouse, promise her I'd go home to Arizona on the next train, promise her that I'd be back to see her the following summer and every summer after that.

An hour passed. I walked from one end of the bridge to the other. I tossed a few rocks over the side. I counted bars in the railing. I looked for shooting stars. I listed all the reasons why I shouldn't have anything to do with that trial.

Naomi never showed up that night, and I was left alone with nothing but my own conscience to help me decide what to do. Right then I wished I was back in Tempe. I wished I had never come to Greenwood, never gotten mixed up with R.C. or Emmett or any of this mess.

One of the last things Mom had said to me on the phone was: "Remember who you are, Hiram, and remember to do what's right."

Who was I?

Hiram Hillburn, a kid from Arizona. Son to an English professor who hated everything about the South, grandson to a gentleman farmer who loved everything about it. Both men had heads harder than cement, and both charged ahead full speed with whatever they thought was right. What they had in common is what kept them apart.

Mr. Paul had told me to use my head, so I started stacking up the positives against the negatives. I knew I could get out of the trial if I really wanted to. Sheriff Smith already had his hands full, and I could slip out of town and he probably wouldn't bother to do a thing about it. The paper had made it pretty clear that both the defense and the prosecution had already lined up witnesses, and neither one had talked to me yet, so I probably wasn't in either side's game plan. And the sooner I left Greenwood, the sooner I'd be back in school, the less homework I'd have to make up. And I could start smoothing things out with Dad.

If I stuck around for the trial, I'd be wasting my time. I'd be in the way. Nothing would get accomplished. Nothing would get changed.

The positives outweighed the negatives by a ton. Now all I had to do was go home and call Mom and Dad to tell them I was coming home as soon as I could. Everybody would be glad: me, Grampa, Naomi, R.C. and his buddies, Mom, and probably even Dad. So it was settled: I'd run away from the trial.

But it wasn't settled. That knot in my stomach didn't go away; it got worse, almost making me want to puke over the bridge rail. All the positives in the world couldn't fool me. I knew what was right, and I knew if I was going to do what was right, I had to show up at the trial and if asked, tell everything I knew. A boy—a boy I knew—had been kidnapped and murdered. And I knew who did it, at least I knew one of the people who had a part in it. Nothing would bring Emmett back to life, but the trial of his killers might be the start of things, might be a small step to making life for Negroes in the South—heck, in the whole United States—a little better. If nothing else, it might make *me* feel a little better.

I was Hiram Hillburn, and I knew what I was going to do: I was going to do what was right.

CHAPTER 14

The Tallahatchie County Courthouse sits smack in the middle of the town square of Sumner, a little town north of Greenwood, and you can tell that when it was built, people figured it had to last till doomsday. The building is three stories of solid brick with long windows on the first and second floors that have solid steel shutters that could be closed in case of atomic bomb blasts, riots, or invasion. Shops and a handful of cafés surround the courthouse. The rest of Sumner isn't much more than a few streets lined with the small houses of townspeople and retired farmers.

Early Monday morning, Grampa and I drove up to Sumner. We were both bleary-eyed and quiet because we'd been up late Sunday night arguing about whether or not I should tell everything if I got called on to testify. Around midnight when Grampa finally realized I wasn't going to change my mind, he swore softly and said, "You're getting to be more like your daddy every day."

"And like you," I said. "I'm like Dad and like you. Stubbornness runs deep in Hillburns."

Grampa shook his head without smiling. "Well, then, Hiram Hillburn, we better be getting ourselves to bed. You may be going to that trial, but you're not going alone, and if we don't leave early, we'll end up parking in Webb and hiking the last two miles to Sumner."

"You sure you want to do this, son?" he asked before I went upstairs.

"As far as I'm concerned, I've got no choice," I said.

The morning air felt hot and heavy, more like August than September, and low, thick clouds dotted the Delta sky. Outside of Greenwood, the sun cast patches of light and shadows across the cotton fields revealing a thin gray mist, unstirred by morning breezes, that clung to the tops of the cotton plants.

For most of the way up Highway 49 into Tallahatchie County, Grampa sat like a man going to his own funeral. I couldn't tell if he was tired or mad; I didn't feel like talking to him, so I just concentrated on keeping the old pickup headed north.

The highway started filling up with traffic before we even got to Webb, and by the time we made it to the little cotton gin town outside of Sumner, we were backed up behind a long line of cars headed for the trial. "Knew there'd be a herd of people coming to this," Grampa muttered.

As we got closer to Sumner, Grampa got more and more uncomfortable. He kept shifting in his seat, rolling his window up, then down again, turning around to look at the cars behind us. At one point he blew air out of his mouth and said, "You know, Hiram, neither one of us got any business being here. We could be setting in the comfort of our home enjoying Ruthanne's fine breakfast. Instead, we're up here in this, this . . . *mob*."

When we finally reached the edge of town, the streets around the courthouse were so crowded that the local sheriff had blocked off the town square and was directing cars to the side streets beyond the square. Grampa, swearing and slapping his hand on the dashboard every time traffic got too tight, directed me to a back street a couple blocks from the square. We parked across a bayou east of the courthouse and walked over the bayou bridge and into the crowd waiting for the trial to begin.

From the sounds of their voices, I could tell most of them were local people, but on one corner of the square an NBC-TV camera had been set up; scattered through the crowd, reporters and photographers were talking to people and snapping flash photographs. Everyone near us was white, but closer to the front of the courthouse a large group of Negroes gathered in the street kitty-corner from the entrance, and even though the streets around the town square were packed with people standing shoulder to shoulder, a clear space separated the Negroes from everyone else.

Around eight o'clock a heavy policeman came out of the main doors and stood on the steps, looking over the crowd.

When he spotted the Negroes, he lifted a bullhorn to his mouth and started talking in their direction.

"Listen here. Listen here! Let me have ya'll's attention." The crowd quieted down. "I'm H. C. Strider, sheriff of Talla- hatchie County, and I'm under the direction of Judge Curtis L. Swango to make sure things stay orderly. Ya'll been waiting a while, and you're gonna be waiting a little more yet. We can't sit but about three hundred people in the courtroom, so the judge wants family and subpoenaed wit- nesses to enter first. Then the press—if you've got proper credentials. After that, it's first come, first serve. Coloreds come last, of course. We got three benches for them set up in back." He looked at the group of Negroes and his eyes narrowed. "Don't want no trouble here, won't tolerate none." Then to the main crowd he said, "All right, folks, we'll be opening the doors shortly," and stepped back inside, clos- ing the doors behind him.

The crowd swelled forward moments later when two deputies opened the doors. "Ya'll hold on now," shouted one. "Family and subpoenaed witnesses first. Step on back and let 'em get up here." People grumbled but let us through. Two women with some young children went in first, then some white men, each holding up his subpoena for the deputy. One of the deputies checked my subpoena and let me and Grampa in. Five or six Negroes came in after us, heads down, trying to look invisible.

When we were all inside, a deputy led us upstairs to the courtroom and searched everyone before we could go in. The deputy told me and Grampa to sit up front on the right side of the room; it'd be a good place to see everything and they'd know where to find me if they wanted me to testify.

Trial hadn't even started, but the room felt like an oven, and as people came in behind us, they started fanning themselves right away. By 9:00 A.M., the courtroom was packed. All the regular seats were taken, so deputies brought in more chairs to line the aisles and the walls. Three wooden benches were pushed up near the back, and when the room looked packed enough to explode, a deputy led a group of Negroes in and directed them to sit there. The benches filled up fast, and those who didn't get a seat had to stand outside in the hallway.

When it looked like everyone who was going to get a seat had one, there was a commotion outside the courtroom door. Somebody said, "I'm Charles C. Diggs, elected congressman from the state of Michigan, and I insist on being given a seat in the courtroom." He argued with somebody for a moment, and then a deputy stuck his head in the doorway and called to an officer inside the courtroom, "There's a nigger here who says he's a congressman."

"A nigger congressman?"

"That's what this nigger said."

The deputy laughed. "Hell, that ain't even legal."

A Negro man in a dark suit appeared in the doorway and flashed something from his wallet to one of the deputies, who looked at it a moment, shook his head, and pointed to the benches inside the door. "Set over there with the other niggers, and don't give us no more trouble."

I'd expected the courtroom to be quiet and serious, like a church, but the crowd buzzed like they were waiting for a carnival to start. A few people smoked cigarettes, and some, only the white people, sipped ice water the deputies had brought in. The Negroes talked quietly among themselves. Grampa guessed about 300 people were sitting there waiting for the trial to begin; I counted only thirty-five Negroes, and most of them looked like they'd rather be anywhere but sitting in a hostile courtroom.

That first day of the trial wasn't a trial at all. We just sat and watched the district attorney, Gerald Chatham, and his assistant argue with the defense lawyers over who'd be on the jury. The main lawyer for Bryant and Milam was J. J. Breland, an attorney from Sumner who Grampa knew from some previous dealings. "Good man," Grampa said. "Knows the law inside and out, and he's a Southerner born and bred." He had a whole army of assistants, Mr. Carlton, Mr. Kellum, and a few more that Grampa didn't know.

Mr. Chatham started the questioning by announcing to everyone, "This case has received wide publicity. The state is going to take every precaution to see that we have a fair and impartial jury." Most everybody nodded, but I heard some people whisper and chuckle, and when they did, Judge Swango was on them like a rattlesnake. He banged his gavel on his desk and said, plenty loud, "We'll have none of that here—not today, not until this trial's over. You people who can't be respectful of the law might just as well leave now, because if I hear any more nonsense, I'll have the bailiff throw you out."

The room got quiet right away, and Mr. Chatham waited before talking. He looked at the judge and then at the men waiting to be interviewed and said, "I'm not going to give the prospective jurors a chance to disqualify themselves because they don't believe in a death sentence," and as soon as he said it, almost everyone in the room started talking while Judge Swango banged his gavel again. It took a minute or two, but as soon as it was quiet again, Mr. Chatham cleared his voice and said, "The state will not seek the death penalty in this case." Grampa didn't look surprised at all, but I couldn't believe it. No death penalty for kidnapping and murder? What kind of trial was this going to be?

Then the interviews began. As a prospective juror stood to be questioned, Mr. Chatham asked the same things over and over: "Would you be prejudiced because of race? Did you contribute to the fund for the defense, or would you contribute if you were asked to?"

Mr. Breland had his own set of questions for each man. "There's been a whole lot of publicity about the alleged events regarding this Emmett Till boy. Will you let that in any way influence you?" If the man said no, Mr. Breland then asked, "If you decide to convict, will you be sure beyond *a reasonable doubt* that the dead body found in the river was the body of Emmett Louis Till?"

The whole time the questioning was going on, Roy Bryant and J. W. Milam sat at a wooden table in the front of the courtroom. Milam, a big man who was mostly bald, looked about ten years older than Bryant. They each had one of their little sons on their laps, and when one of the boys got fussy, they'd hand him over their shoulder to their wives, who sat in the row of chairs just behind them. Watching them sit there playing with their sons, reading the paper, smoking, or drinking a Coke, I never would have guessed they were on trial for murder. Once in a while they'd talk to each other or point out something in the newspaper they had spread on the table in front of them, but neither one ever said anything to their lawyers or paid any attention to what was going on.

After a couple hours of watching both sides interview white men for the jury, Grampa leaned over and nudged me. "J.J. really knows how to work the law, doesn't he? That old Chatham doesn't have a chance, not one chance in hell."

"You think he's ever going to interview any women?"

"Women can't be on juries in Mississippi," Grampa said.

"What about Negroes?"

"You've got to be a registered voter to be called into a jury pool, and Negroes don't like to vote in the Delta, so none of them ever bother to register."

"Why don't they want to vote?"

Grampa answered without looking at me. "That's just the way things are down here."

During the noon recess Grampa bought me lunch at a crowded café across the street from the courthouse. Neither one of us had eaten breakfast, so we inhaled the chicken salad sandwiches and potato chips Grampa ordered. After we each had a piece of pie, Grampa leaned back and sighed. "I can't help but feel like we're wasting our time up here, Hiram. Chatham's not cooperating at all. If he'd just go along with J. J. Breland, they'd have had that jury picked and seated before lunch." He looked at me carefully. "You still sure you want to stick around for all this?"

I wondered that myself. At the rate the morning had gone, this trial might last for weeks, and I wasn't sure how long I wanted to sit there sweating about being called up to testify. But when I thought about what had happened to Emmett Till, that old Hillburn stubbornness kicked in. "I'm staying until the trial's over, but you don't have to come back, Grampa. There's no good reason for you to be here."

He pulled out his wallet to pay for lunch. "I got my reasons," he said. And under his breath he muttered, "Too many damn reasons for my own good."

Grampa's reaction surprised me. I had thought that all his fuss about me being at the trial was because he was worried about me, but now I wasn't sure why he didn't want me mixed up in the trial.

On the way out of the café, Grampa stuffed a few dollar bills into a fruit jar labeled "Bryant and Milam Defense Fund: Contributions Welcome" on a table by the door.

The jar overflowed with money.

When settled into our courtroom seats Tuesday morning, we figured to see the jury selection get finished and the trial begin. We hadn't been sitting very long when there was some talking and moving out in the hallway. A moment later a well-dressed Negro woman about Mom's age came in, and the Negro congressman and another man led her to the benches in the back. When the Negroes sitting there saw her, they all stood up, and a few women hugged her and some others started crying.

"The nigger boy's mama," someone said. "Come down from Chicago." It didn't take long for the word to spread around the courtroom, and pretty soon white people were turning around in their seats staring at her, mean, hateful stares.

A minute later Sheriff Strider pushed through the crowd, walked back to the Negro benches and handed her an envelope. "You've been served," he said without looking at her. "Don't leave the area without notifying the court."

She only nodded and sat down.

Tuesday morning dragged like Monday had, but finally, after the lawyers had interviewed more than 100 white men, Judge Swango ordered the twelve jurors and one alternate to sit in a group of chairs on his right and gave them instructions, stuff we'd all heard several times from the lawyers. When he finished, he announced that the trial would be postponed until Wednesday morning because the prosecution and the defense wanted to interview surprise witnesses the prosecution had just subpoenaed. Then he rapped his gavel on his desk and left the courtroom.

A few people applauded, and everybody except me started talking all excited about what had happened so far and what would be next.

I didn't want to think about it, but I knew everything would start tomorrow.

After supper that night I wanted to go out and see if Naomi might be waiting by the bridge, but Grampa wouldn't let me. "There's trouble brewing, son. This trial's got people riled up, and no telling what some hothead might do, especially if he knows you're on the potential witness list."

I knew he was talking about R.C., but I didn't say anything.

"Best thing for you to do is stay inside, listen to the radio or read a while, and then get to bed. Tomorrow'll be a long day, and even though the paper says both sides want a fast trial, we might be wrapped up in this a lot longer than either of us wants to be."

"You think I'll have to testify?"

Grampa shrugged. "You're on their list. Are you still willing?"

"I never wanted to, but I will if I have to."

"You're letting a bunch of knucklehead lawyers decide what's going to happen to you, Hiram." Grampa's voice shook, and his face turned red. "A man's got to take charge of his own life. He's got to do what he thinks is right."

I didn't remind him, but that's exactly what I was doing.

Wednesday morning the courtroom was noisier, hotter, and more crowded than ever. The judge reminded us all to behave ourselves and chewed out a couple of photographers for taking pictures in the courtroom; then the trial began.

Mr. Chatham went first. He faced the jury and said, "The

state has found six new witnesses who will place the defendants"—he pointed at Bryant and Milam—"with the Negro boy several hours after he was taken from Mose Wright's shack. These witnesses will present absolutely newly discovered evidence that will convince you, beyond a shadow of a doubt, that Roy Bryant and J. W. Milam kidnapped and murdered the child named Emmett Till."

The first witness was Emmett's uncle, Mose Wright, a poor sharecropper and part-time minister from Money. The courtroom was so packed with spectators that the small old Negro man had to push his way through the crowd to get to the witness chair. The chair was almost too big for him, and he sat at the edge of it, uncomfortable. After he sat down, Bryant and Milam glared at him for a moment, and then they sat back and ignored him.

Mr. Chatham approached the witness chair like he thought a fast move might scare Mose Wright out of there. "Uncle Mose," he said, "what was your relationship with the deceased child?"

"Bobo Till was my nephew." His voice was clear and strong; not a hint of fear in it. "He come down from Chicago to visit family for a spell."

"Tell us what happened early on the morning of Sunday, August twenty-eighth."

Mose Wright straightened up, looked at Bryant and Milam, and then at Mr. Chatham. "'Bout two o'clock somebody come pounding at the door. They said, 'Preacher, Preacher.' One of 'em said, 'This is Mr. Bryant.' I got up and opened the door. Mr. Milam was standing at the door with a pistol in his right hand and a flashlight in d'other."

"Uncle Mose," said Mr. Chatham, "do you see Mr. Milam in the courtroom?"

Nobody moved, not even the children who had been playing on Bryant's and Milam's laps. It felt like everybody was holding their breath, waiting for a bomb to go off.

Mose Wright stood up from his chair and pointed a knobby finger at J. W. Milam. "There he is."

Everyone who'd been holding their breath let it out all at once and started talking. Someone shouted "Lyin' nigger!" and "Lynch him!" A woman moaned. Somebody was crying. It took Judge Swango a lot of pounding and shouting to get things orderly again.

While all this was happening, Mose Wright stood as calm as Jesus on stormy water, like he couldn't see or hear the hell that had broken loose in Judge Swango's courtroom. When the judge had the room quiet again, Mr. Chatham walked up to the witness chair and rested one hand on the armrest.

"Uncle Mose, do you see the other man who was on the porch that night?"

"Yessuh. That's him there." He pointed at Bryant.

"Mr. Roy Bryant?"

"Yessuh."

"Objection!" J. J. Breland jumped to his feet. "Objection! Your Honor, I object to this wild unsubstantiated testimony." Mr. Breland looked ready to deliver a speech, but Judge Swango stopped him in mid-sentence.

"Overruled. You'll have your chance to cross-examine."

Mr. Chatham nodded to the judge, and then turned back to his witness. "What happened next, Uncle Mose?"

"Well, Mr. Milam had that pistol, and he asked me if I had the boy out of Chicago. Then one of the men said, 'I wants that boy who done that talk at Money.' They shoved past me and went looking in the back bedrooms, and a minute later they dragged Bobo from his room, shaking him and sayin' hateful things. Poor old Bobo was a-tryin' to get dressed as they dragged him to the front door.

"I was scared. I didn't want them hurtin' my nephew, so I asked them what they was going to do with the boy, and Mr. Milam, he said, 'If he's not the right boy, we are going to bring him back and put him in bed.'

"Before they got to the door, one of the men asked me how old I was, and I tol' him sixty-four, and he said, 'You better not cause any trouble, Preacher, or you'll never live to be sixty-five.'

"By then my wife heard all the fuss and come outta the bedroom a-cryin' and beggin' them to leave the boy home. That made the men real mad and one of them hollered, 'You git back in the bed, and I want to hear those springs.' My wife said, 'Listen, we'll pay you whatever you want if you release him,' but they just ignored her.

"I stayed on the porch while they dragged Bobo out to their car. They hit him a couple times to make him stop complaining. The car didn't have no lights on, and they pulled Bobo up to the back door and asked somebody inside, 'Is this the boy?' and somebody said, 'Yes.'"

"Was that a man's voice or a woman's?" Mr. Chatham asked.

Mose Wright shifted in his seat. "It seemed lighter than a man's."

"Was there anyone else in the car?"

"Yessuh. Looked to me like a man was sitting in the back-seat along with her."

"What happened next, Uncle?"

"I heard them slap the boy a few more times, heard him cry out. Heard car doors open and close; then they drove away with the lights still off." His face turned sad. "Didn't never see the boy alive again."

"Were you at the Tallahatchie River when a body was pulled out three days later?"

"Yessuh."

"Did you identify the body?" Chatham asked.

"It was Bobo, Emmett Till. I watched the sheriff and his helpers pull him out of the water, and I got a good look at him. He had no face hair—Bobo never did have no face hair on him—and the boy didn't have no clothes on, but they did find a ring on one of his fingers, with the initials L.T. on it."

Mr. Chatham turned to face the jury. "You saw the ring?" he asked without looking at Mose.

"Yessuh. Exact same ring the boy's daddy, Louis Till, used to wear. I seen it on Bobo many times."

Mr. Chatham nodded at the men in the jury, then said, "No further questions, Your Honor."

As soon as Mr. Chatham sat down, J. J. Breland jumped

out of his seat to start questioning. "Mose, you got a porch light on that old shack of yours?"

"Nosuh."

"So at two a.m. things would be pretty dark out there?"

"I reckon so."

"Didn't you tell defense lawyers that the only reason you thought it was Mr. Milam at the door was because he was big and bald?"

Mose sat silent.

"All you saw was a bald-headed man?"

"That's right."

"And had you ever seen Mr. Milam or Mr. Bryant before that night you claim the boy was kidnapped?"

"Nosuh."

"Was there ever any light turned on in the house?"

"Nosuh."

"Did you ever see the flashlight shine in Mr. Bryant's face that night?"

"I could see him good enough."

"So, old Mose, it was completely dark inside and out, and the only light came from a flashlight, a flashlight shining directly in your face." Mr. Breland grinned and shook his head. "And yet you could see clearly, clearly enough to accuse two *white* men of murder, to claim that the men on your porch were Mr. Bryant and Mr. Milam over there. Could have been any two men, white or black, for all you could see, Mose." He looked at Mose, his smile gone now. "You got a problem with white people, Mose? Are you trying to even some old score?"

Mose didn't answer.

"You hear me, boy? Do you have a problem with white people?"

"No."

"No problem with white folks, yet there you sit accusing two of our upstanding white citizens of barging into your home in the middle of the night, pointing a gun and a flashlight in your face, and hauling off your nephew. That sounds pretty far-fetched to me, Mose. Does it to you?"

Mose looked him in the eye and swallowed before answering. "No, it don't. It's what happened, and that's God's honest truth."

Mr. Breland smiled again. "The state's only eyewitness to this 'crime' is an old man seeing things in the dark. Wonder what those other surprise witnesses have seen. I tell you what, Mose, this sure is somebody's kind of truth, but I wouldn't be ascribing it to God." People in the courtroom laughed and somebody shouted something, but Judge Swango quieted them all down by pounding his gavel. Mr. Breland shook his head like a little kid in trouble and sat down.

Next Mr. Chatham called Sheriff Smith to the stand. When I heard his name, my stomach about dropped right out of me. Was I next? Would the sheriff tell what I had told him about R.C.? I shivered as he was sworn in.

As soon as Sheriff Smith sat down, Mr. Breland stood up. "Objection, Your Honor. We object to this witness and insist the jury be excused until we can see if this witness is qualified to testify as to facts pertinent to this case."

"Sustained," the judge said, and while the jury moved out of the courtroom, Sheriff Smith shifted uncomfortably on the stand.

"Proceed with your questions, Mr. Chatham," the judge said when the jurors were gone.

"Sheriff, I believe that early on the morning after Emmett Till's abduction, you arrested Milam and Bryant on suspicion of kidnapping."

"That's right."

"And what did they tell you when you picked them up?"

"Well, sir, they admitted they had kidnapped the boy. Mr. Bryant, he said he went down there to Mose Wright's house and brought the boy up to his store in Money, and he wasn't the right boy, the one who did the talking and the whistling, and he turned him loose."

"So they confessed to you, Sheriff, that they had kidnapped Emmett Till?"

"Yessir."

"No further questions, Your Honor."

Mr. Breland stood up. "Your Honor, this testimony has no relevance to the charges of murder for which this court is convened, and I move that it be disallowed from jury and the trial records."

Judge Swango thought a moment and said, "So granted." When Mr. Chatham stood to complain, the judge motioned for him to sit back down. "The state must first prove Emmett Till was murdered. The only proof is that the boy is missing. There's no evidence of criminal homicide. You can step down, Sheriff."

When Sheriff Smith left the witness stand, I let out a sigh of relief. If his testimony wasn't relevant, mine probably wasn't going to be either.

When the jury came back in, the next witness was Chester Miller, a Negro undertaker who had helped with Emmett's body when it was pulled out of the Tallahatchie. "It was a Negro boy, for sure," he told Mr. Chatham, "bruised and beat up something awful. The whole top of his head was crushed in so bad that a piece of his skull bone fell out in the boat when they pulled him out of the water."

"Was there a ring with the initials L.T. on the boy's hand?" Mr. Chatham asked.

"Yessuh."

Mr. Chatham thanked him and sat down.

Chester Miller looked scared when Mr. Breland started questioning him. Before he asked his first question, Mr. Breland stood in front of the witness chair and stared at him for a few seconds. Then he asked, in a real loud voice, "Chester, what kind of training do you have?"

He looked confused and said nothing.

"I mean, what qualifications do you have?"

Chester stared into his lap, barely breathing.

"Lookit here, boy"—Mr. Breland's voice turned mean— "you've got to answer me when I talk to you!"

"Y-yessuh."

"Do you have any medical or undertaking training?"

"Ain't never been to a doctor, suh."

The audience snickered, and Mr. Breland turned and looked at us like a teacher who just doesn't know what to do with a dumb student. He turned sideways and sighed. "Chester, can you tell me what you do for a living?"

"Collect folks' dead ones and get 'em buried."

"So you're a mortician?"

Again Chester looked confused.

"An undertaker?"

"Yessuh."

"Chester, when you first saw this body, did you recognize it? Was it Emmett Till?"

"Well, his head was beaten up pretty bad, so it'd a been hard to tell right off who it was no matter what, but—"

Breland interrupted him. "When you first inspected it, did you or did you not know the body was that of Emmett Till?"

"I never knowed the Till boy," Chester said softly, "so right then, without a picture or a family member, there'd a been no way to tell—"

"So," Breland said impatiently, "you were never able to make a positive identification of this body." Then, in a kind voice, he asked, "You didn't know who it was, but did you determine the exact cause of death?"

"Nosuh. I couldn't tell any one thing for sure. The boy's body had bruises and cuts all over, and his head was pretty much caved in, from a beatin' and being shot, I guess. And somebody had wired an ol' pulley around his neck. And there was one other thing." He paused and stared at the floor, nervous and embarrassed. "The boy's manhood'd been cut clean off."

Hearing what had happened to Emmett chilled me to the bone, and I would have been sick if I hadn't seen the look on Mr. Breland's face. The description of Emmett's corpse didn't even faze him; you could tell he didn't care a hoot about this Negro boy who'd been tortured and murdered. I wanted to jump up and scream at him, at all the hardheaded, heartless people in the room.

"Have you ever been to a school for undertakers, Chester?" Mr. Breland looked irritated. "Have you had any training, an apprenticeship in the mortuary profession?"

Chester paused. Finally he said, "Nosuh. I ain't never been to no school."

Breland nodded, and with his hands folded behind his back he walked over to face the jury.

He looked like he was trying not to laugh. "No, of course you wouldn't have," he said almost to himself. "So, other than the experience you have collecting dead folks, you really have no expertise at all to make a positive or scientific identification of a corpse. You see"—he swept his arm from the jury to the witness chair—"even one of their own cannot testify with a surety as to the identity of the body that was pulled from the Tallahatchie River."

The next witness was Sheriff Strider, who had also been at the river when Emmett's body was pulled out. When Mr. Chatham asked him if he knew the cause of death, the sheriff looked smug and said, "He had a bullet hole just above the ear."

I closed my eyes and squeezed the armrests of my chair;

I didn't want to think about the awful stuff that had happened to Emmett.

Mr. Chatham thanked him and sat down. Then Mr. Breland said to Sheriff Strider, "Sheriff, sounds to me like you know more about undertaking than some folks around here." The courtroom audience laughed, and Judge Swango pounded his gavel again. Mr. Breland looked up at the judge with a kind of "I couldn't help it" smile, and then asked the sheriff to describe the body.

"Well, he sure was dead," he said with a grin, then seeing that no one laughed, continued. "Shot to the head. Looked to have been in the water at least ten days, maybe a couple weeks or more. A big old cotton gin pulley had been tied round his neck with barbed wire. Whoever dropped that body in the river sure didn't want it floating up any time soon."

"Did you notice anything in particular about this corpse, anything that could help identify it?"

"All I could tell about that body was that it was human; it was in such bad shape, I couldn't even be sure if it was white or Negro." He looked at Mr. Breland, waiting for another question, but Mr. Breland said nothing, so the sheriff continued. "You know, there's some folks, some groups, rabble-rousers and the kind, that would do anything to stir up trouble down here. They're bent on disrupting our way of life, and I wouldn't put it past them killing somebody, sticking some boy's ring on him, and throwing his body in the river. Could be that Till boy is right now sitting in Chicago or somewhere up north having a good old time with all this trouble going on down here.

"No, sir, that body'd been in the water a good two weeks, long before that Negro boy got himself kidnapped. The corpse they pulled out the Tallahatchie was no more Emmett Till than I'm a jackass."

When Emmett Till's mother walked up to the witness chair, I was afraid people in the courtroom were going to jump out of their seats and knock her down. Looks of hate, pure meanness, followed her all the way to the stand, and I wondered, if we hadn't been in a courtroom full of police, would some people have hauled her out and lynched her?

She spoke clearly, and she didn't look either scared or mad, just kind of sad, like she was still hurting something awful for Emmett.

"Emmett was born and raised in Chicago," she told Mr. Chatham, "so he didn't know how to be humble to white people. I warned him before he came down here; I told him to be very careful how he spoke and to say 'yes, sir' and 'no, ma'am' and not to hesitate to humble himself if he had to get down on his knees."

Mr. Chatham looked sympathetic. "Mrs. Bradley, when your son's body arrived in Chicago, were you able to identify it as him?"

"Yes, sir, positively."

"How did you do that?"

"A mother knows her child, has known him since he was born. I looked at the face very carefully . . . I just looked at it very carefully, and I was able to find out that it was my son, Emmett Louis Till."

Mr. Chatham went to his table, picked up a large photograph, and walked back in front of Emmett's mother. "Mrs. Bradley, I have a photograph here, taken at the Century Burial Association, of the body that was removed from the Tallahatchie River on August thirty-first. I'd like you to look at it and tell me if you can identify this body."

He handed her the picture. Her face became even more somber as she looked at it and nodded; then handed it back to Mr. Chatham. "That's my son," she said softly, "my son, Emmett Till." Her voice broke, and she took off her glasses to wipe away tears.

"Are you sure?" Mr. Chatham asked gently.

"If I thought it wasn't my boy, I would be out looking for him now."

I could hardly stand to look at Emmett's mother, and I prayed she wouldn't look at me. I was afraid if she did that, I'd just fall apart crying, that I'd confess all the things I didn't do, things I might have done that could've saved Emmett. I'd stand up and shout to the judge, jury, and everybody in the courtroom that R. C. Rydell had been a part of this, that he told me he was going to do something. But she never did look at me, never even glanced in my direction.

The next witness was Willie Reed, a Negro kid about my age. He was so scared that he could hardly talk, and Judge Swango had to keep telling him to speak up so the jury could hear. It looked to me like Willie didn't want anybody to hear him, didn't want anything at all to do with this trial, but as I listened to him tell what he had seen and heard after Emmett had been kidnapped, I admired him. As a Negro testifying against two white men, he'd never be able to stay in Mississippi, probably never even be able to visit here again. He had a lot more guts than I did.

When Willie said that he saw some white men in a blue Ford pickup with Emmett Till in the back, Grampa's breathing started getting noisy. His face turned fish-belly white, and sweat poured off his forehead. He didn't even notice me looking at him, so I touched his arm and said, "Grampa, you okay? You didn't forget your medicine this morning did you?"

Grampa looked at me glassy-eyed, like he'd just come out of a dream.

"Are you feeling all right?" I asked. It looked like maybe his diabetes was acting up; I hoped it wasn't another stroke. "Do you need a drink or something?"

"That Sunday morning, you fixed us breakfast," he said, his voice raspy, "and we played cards, remember?"

"Yessir. Stayed home all morning because neither one of us felt any good."

"That's right. Yes, of course, that's right." I had no idea what he was talking about, but whatever had hit him must have passed, because the color came back into his face. "I'm fine, son," he said quietly. "Just been sitting in this hot old courtroom for too long." He sat up straighter and looked at the witness stand real serious, like he was trying to hear every word.

Willie Reed was talking about how he saw some white men come out of a barn, a barn on the plantation owned by Leslie Milam, J.W.'s brother. "I heard someone getting licked pretty good inside there, and lots of crying. After some more licking, he cried, 'Mama, Lord have mercy. Lord have mercy!' and I went running to my aunt's house to ask who was gettin' beat over in the barn."

"Did you recognize any of the men?" asked Mr. Chatham.

"Mr. J. W. Milam. I saw him leave the barn and get a drink from the well and then go back inside."

"Objection!" shouted Mr. Breland. "Your Honor, I object to this witness!"

"Grounds?" asked the judge.

"This testimony does not officially connect my clients with whatever was going on in that barn. This witness is merely speculating about what might or might not have happened."

"Overruled," said the judge. "Continue your questioning, Mr. Chatham."

Mr. Chatham nodded to the judge. "Willie, did you notice anything else about Mr. Milam when you saw him outside that barn?"

"He was wearing a pistol, had it strapped in a holster on his hip."

"Objection! Objection!" Mr. Breland was on his feet this time. I didn't hear all that he said, because I was still worried about Grampa. His breathing had gotten easier, but he was fidgeting in his chair now; he couldn't seem to get comfortable. The judge overruled whatever it was Mr. Breland had been complaining about, and Mr. Chatham asked Willie Reed another question.

"What did you do next?"

"I went to the country store to get some things; then I went home and got ready for Sunday school."

"On the way back, did you see or hear anything or anybody?"

"Nosuh."

"Was the pickup gone?"

"Yessuh."

When Mr. Breland had his turn to ask Willie questions, he looked like a bull about to rip into a poor old farmer, and Willie looked scared. "Do you know Mr. J. W. Milam?" he asked.

"Nosuh, but I've seen him round the plantation three or four times."

"Have you seen that blue Ford pickup before?"

"Nosuh."

"Then you can't say for sure that it belongs to either of my clients, is that right?"

"Yessuh."

"Did you see Mr. J. W. Milam driving the truck?"

Willie shifted in his chair, looking more and more nervous. "I don't know, suh."

"You wouldn't say Mr. Milam was inside the truck?"

"Nosuh, I wouldn't."

Hearing that made Mr. Breland loosen up a little. "Willie, how far were you from the barn when you saw who you thought was Mr. Milam?"

"Don't know, suh. . . . A ways away."

"A ways? How far exactly is 'a ways'?"

Willie didn't answer.

Mr. Breland turned and pointed to the back of the courtroom. "Is 'a ways' from where you sit to the courtroom doors?"

"Nosuh."

"Farther?"

Willie nodded.

"Twice as far?"

"Don't know, suh. I wasn't thinking about the distance at the time."

"Well, boy, what were you thinking about? If you weren't thinking, how in the world can you be so sure you saw who you claim you saw?"

Again Willie said nothing.

"Think hard, boy. From where you were standing when you heard the licking and the hollering, how far is it to the barn? One hundred yards? Two hundred? Three hundred? Think, boy! You're sitting in a court of law, sworn to testify in front of these good people, and we're all waiting for your answer. C'mon, Willie!"

Willie mumbled something too softly to be heard.

"Speak up, boy," said Mr. Breland.

Willie looked embarrassed and confused. "Guess maybe it was round four hundred yards."

"Four hundred yards?" Mr. Breland whistled. "That's nearly a quarter of a mile. You've got yourself a damn good set of eyes, boy. Better get yourself off to Korea and let the Army use you as a sharpshooter."

Willie tried to say something more, but Mr. Breland wouldn't let him. "You're done. Just go set down for a while."

Looking relieved, Willie left the witness chair and walked straight out of the courtroom without once looking up. After Willie was gone, Mr. Chatham looked down at the papers spread out on the table in front of him like he was hoping to find something he'd forgotten or overlooked.

"Does the state have any more witnesses?" Judge Swango had to ask him twice before he finally looked up. Mr. Chatham rose slowly and glanced around the courtroom. Then he looked at the judge and said, "No, Your Honor. The state rests."

Mr. Breland and his lawyers smiled when they heard that. A couple of his assistants even patted him on the back.

"Does the defense have any witnesses?" asked Judge Swango.

"Mrs. Carolyn Bryant," said Mr. Breland.

Mrs. Bryant, a pretty young woman, patted her husband on the shoulder and stepped around him to walk up to the witness seat. Mr. Breland made a big show of acting like a gentleman and helped her get seated; then he asked her to tell what had happened to her at her husband's store in Money on the night of August 24.

Before she could start talking, though, Judge Swango dismissed the jury. "This event happened too long before the abduction of Emmett Till," he said. "It is not immediately relevant to this case and may prejudice the jury's deliberations. However, I will direct that it be entered into the court record."

Mrs. Bryant smiled shyly at the judge and waited until the jury had left the room. She kept shifting in the witness stand, not sure where to put her hands, not sure where to look. When she made eye contact with her husband, she nodded and stopped fidgeting, and that's when I remembered what the paper had first reported about the kidnapping; there had been three men and a *woman* in the car that night.

She told Mr. Breland that she had been working in their store alone because her husband was on a business trip. "While I was working, a Negro boy came into the store and stopped at the candy counter. I noticed that he spoke with a Northern brogue. He ordered some bubble gum, and when I held out my right hand for some money"—she shivered— "he caught my hand and wouldn't let go. I tried to pull my hand away, and he said, 'How about a date, baby?'"

The courtroom had been deadly silent, but then a woman gasped, and I heard muttered swearing. A man behind me said, "No wonder that nigger ended up in the river. I hope they made him pay good before they tossed him in."

The evil emotion in the room almost choked me. Didn't these people know they were talking about a fourteen-year-old boy?

"I shook my hand loose and started to the back of the store. He caught me at the cash register . . ." Her voice shook. "And he put both hands around my waist. He said, 'What's the matter, baby, can't you take it?' I pulled myself away from him, and all the while he was saying filthy, unprintable words, words which I will not repeat. Then he said, 'I've been with white women before.'"

The murmur in the courtroom grew louder, and Judge Swango banged on his desk to quiet everyone down. Mrs. Bryant waited until the judge signaled her to continue.

"Then another Negro came in and pulled him out of the store. I started to go to the car to get my pistol, and he was still on the front porch of the store. He smiled and whistled at me, then ran off with his friends, got in a car, and drove away."

"Was this Negro man who accosted you Emmett Till?"

She paused and looked at her husband a moment before answering. "I don't know Emmett Till. I've never known Emmett Till, or any other Negroes, for that matter."

CHAPTER 15

A huge thunderstorm woke us early Friday morning. Lightning lit up the sky, and rain pounded our roof and windows. I had hoped that the morning rain would make the courtroom more bearable, but the rain stopped early, and the humidity it left behind only made the air in Sumner hotter and heavier.

The courtroom was packed that morning. Grampa figured this would be the last day of the trial, and I guess so did everyone else in Mississippi. Deputies brought in extra cane-bottomed chairs and squeezed them in wherever there was floor space. Spectators, newsmen, and photographers jammed the foyer outside the courtroom, and everybody was waiting for something big to happen.

Mr. Breland called a bunch of character witnesses to testify, and each of them said about the same thing. Milam and Bryant had been born and raised in Mississippi. Milam was a war hero. They were good boys, hard workers, and never caused anybody a bit of trouble. When the seventh witness finished, I was just about asleep. Then I heard Mr. Breland tell the judge, "Your Honor, the defense rests."

A few people started clapping until Judge Swango stared them down. He looked at Mr. Chatham and asked, "Is the state prepared for its final argument?"

Mr. Chatham nodded, walked to the jury seats, and faced them, looking at each juror one at a time. When he finished making eye contact, he started speaking so loudly that it made me and Grampa jump in our seats.

He reviewed all the details: the eyewitness testimony of Mose Wright and Willie Reed, the prior confession of Bryant and Milam to kidnapping, the positive identification of the body by Emmett's mother and others. Then he became very serious. He stopped pacing in front of the jury, took a deep breath, and continued with the last part of his speech.

"The first words that entered this case, 'I want the boy from Chicago who did the talking at Money,' were dripping with the blood of Emmett Till. As far as the state of Mississippi is concerned, this is not about race, it's just another murder. But I want to say to you that the murder of Emmett Till was a cowardly act and a brutal and unnecessary killing of a human being. His abduction at gunpoint was unjustified. This was a summary court-martial with the death penalty. That child had done nothing that would cause the defendants to invade the privacy of that home.

"When Bryant and Milam took Emmett Till from the

home of Uncle Mose Wright, they were absolutely and morally responsible for his protection. I was born and bred in the South, and the very worst punishment that should have occurred—if they had any idea in their minds that this boy did anything wrong—was to take a razor strap, turn him over a barrel, and whip him. I've whipped my boy. You've whipped yours. A man deals with a child accordingly as a child, not as a man to a man.

"The killing of Emmett Till was a cowardly act committed by the two defendants you see sitting before you. I know what you are and where we are, but I beg you to put aside race, tradition, and prejudice, and consider the facts of this case that we have so clearly presented. This is not an issue of Negro versus white. This is not an issue of North versus South. This is a simple issue of law: Two men murdered a child. You have no other choice but to convict them for murder."

When he finished speaking, he stayed in front of the jury, looking again into the eyes of each one. Not a single man tried to avoid his gaze.

Then it was J. J. Breland's turn. He walked confidently to the jury, smiled, and, while pointing to Bryant and Milam, said, "I've known those two boys for years. They're men of good reputation, respected businessmen in the community, what I'd call real patriots, one hundred percent Americans.

"This trial has been a waste of the state's time and money. The prosecution talked generalities because the facts just didn't bear out the guilt of these defendants. Where's the motive?" he shouted. "Where's the motive?

"It's plain and simple that the state has no case, no evidence, no identification, no motive. They claimed that Till's wolf-whistle at Mrs. Bryant at her store in Money gave my clients enough reason to kill the boy, but both these men have testified to the authorities that they released the boy, unharmed, after his abduction because they determined he was not the one who had done the whistling. In no way did the state link up the dead boy with these defendants.

"Mrs. Bryant's own testimony did nothing to implicate Till in the incident at her store. She made it clear that Till never had anything to do with her, that she'd never even seen the boy. So why, I ask you, would her husband go out of his way to injure a Negro boy who had committed no offense against him or his family?

"The only testimony that suggested Emmett Till did anything in connection with these defendants was Mose Wright's testimony that he had heard that the boy had done something. However, any fool knows that if Mose had known Emmett Till was involved in something down there, he would have gotten him out and whipped him himself.

"And how could old Mose Wright tell whether the alleged kidnappers were black or white when he had a flashlight shining directly into his face in a completely dark house? It was so dark that night that Mose couldn't even determine the make of the abductors' car. Then he claimed the man identified himself as 'Mr. Bryant.' I ask you, how many Mr. Bryants are there in the state of Mississippi? Had any of you gone to Mose Wright's house with evil intent, would you have given your name? There's nothing reasonable about the state's theory. If that's identification, if that places these men at that scene"—he paused a moment, then shouted each word—"then none of us are safe!

"I wouldn't put it past the NAACP and other Northern rabble-rousers to plant a body in the Tallahatchie River and claim it was Till. There are people in the United States who want to destroy the way of life of Southern people. The state did not prove the body was Till's; it couldn't have been. You heard witnesses, *qualified* professionals, testify that the body had been in the water two weeks or more, while Till had been missing only three days before that body was found. Believe me, there are people who will commit any crime known to man to widen the gap between the white and colored people of the United States. They would not be above putting a rotting, stinking body in the river in the hope it would be identified as Emmett Till.

"My friends, these cold, calculating groups along with the Northern media are doing everything they can to disrupt this trial, to destroy the South. I am sure that every last Anglo-Saxon of you has the courage to free these men in the face of that pressure. We have got to use our legal system to protect our God-given freedoms. If we do not, we have sinned before God and before our fellow citizens of the great state of Mississippi." He paused, and then continued with a quieter, even more serious tone.

"If you convict these two men, it would be admitting that freedom is lost forever. I'll be waiting for you when you come out from your deliberations. If your verdict is guilty, I want you to come to me and tell me where is the land of the free and the home of the brave. I say to you, gentlemen, your forefathers will absolutely turn over in their graves if you don't set these boys loose."

When Mr. Breland finally sat down, the judge sent the jury out of the courtroom to decide whether or not Bryant and Milam were guilty. It seemed like a simple case to me. Mr. Breland's argument was so full of holes that even I could see he didn't have a leg to stand on. There was no doubt that Bryant and Milam were guilty, and I was sure the jury would see it the same way.

A few people left the courtroom, but Grampa and I stayed in that sweatbox and waited. It had been a long week, and Grampa looked exhausted. When the jury was dismissed, we talked a little, but then he dozed off, and I decided to let him sleep. I figured the jury would be out for quite a while.

But barely an hour later they came back in. When the judge asked them if they had a verdict for Bryant and Milam, the foreman stood up. "Yes, sir." He cleared his throat and read from a paper he held. "We find the defendants not guilty."

The words triggered cheering and celebration. Bryant and Milam shook hands and slapped backs with their lawyers; then they turned and kissed their wives. Somebody handed both of them cigars, and Milam lit his up immediately. Now that the trial was over, photographers were free to snap photos, and flashbulbs were going off all over the room. People acted like it was the Fourth of July, and the Korean War had just been declared over.

But in the midst of all that celebrating, I felt like someone had knocked the wind out of me. How could the jury find them innocent? These two men—and others—had murdered a boy, and now their fellow citizens had not only turned them loose but were celebrating. It made me sick, and all I wanted to do was get out of there, out of Mississippi, and back home where things and people weren't so crazy.

Grampa didn't cheer and clap like most white people in the courtroom. As soon as the verdict was announced, he slumped forward and rested his head in his hands. He took several deep breaths, and a few minutes later when he sat up, he looked better, almost relieved that the trial was over. Before we turned to leave, Milam, who was swarmed by reporters and friends, turned, looked right at Grampa, grinned, and gave him the thumbs-up sign.

Grampa acted like he hadn't seen it.

It took a while for the crowd to thin out enough for us to leave the courtroom. When we got to the foyer, an NBC-TV reporter was interviewing Sheriff Strider about the trial. "Is it true," the reporter asked, "that you've been getting hate mail ever since the arrest of Bryant and Milam?"

"I'm glad you asked me this," said the sheriff as he looked into the camera. "I just want to tell all those people who've been sending me threatening letters that if they ever come down here, the same thing's gonna happen to them that happened to Emmett Till."

The reporter asked another question, but by then I was too far down the hall to hear what he said. Besides, I didn't want to hear anything more about this case.

I'd had all I could take.

CHAPTER 16

When we got home that night, Grampa looked awful: His face was washed out, paler than I'd ever seen it. The trial had probably been harder on him than on me, I thought at the time, because he was worried about me testifying in the most spectacular case in the history of Mississippi. Maybe he'd had some threatening letters because of me, letters he'd kept to himself. There's no telling what some nuts would say to an old man whose grandson might testify on the wrong side of a local murder trial.

When we sat down for supper, Grampa sighed. "I am glad that trial's over, gladder than I've been for anything in a long, long time. Maybe we can finally forget about Emmett Till and that mess up in Money."

"You think it's over, Grampa?" I asked. "The trial's the end of it?"

"It's over for those two boys, that's for sure. Once you're acquitted of a crime, you can't be tried for it again."

"But what about the people who helped them?" R. C. Rydell. Would he get away with murder?

"Get that out of your head, Hiram." Grampa's voice sounded strong even though he looked like a good sneeze would knock him right out of his chair. "Just you forget about it. The authorities did a thorough investigation, and there wasn't enough evidence to convict Bryant and Milam. If they'd had a good reason to suspect anyone else—including R. C. Rydell—they would have been after them in a hot minute."

"But the paper said Bryant and Milam weren't alone that night."

Grampa slapped the table with his hand. "Dammitall, Hiram, you ought to be smart enough to know newspapers make mistakes. Rumors are always flying around in cases like these, and the lawyers made it clear that those Negro witnesses lacked reliability."

"But what if Bryant and Milam are covering for somebody else?"

"It's done, Hiram, and believe you me, nobody around here is going to bring up this ugly mess again. It's over. Period."

"What about an appeal? Won't Mr. Chatham take it to another court? Can't he keep fighting it, maybe try to go after the other people involved?" I felt bad complaining to Grampa about the trial after all the worrying he'd done about me, but I couldn't keep quiet about it. "It's just not right, Bryant and Milam getting turned loose. Everybody in that courtroom knew they were guilty; I still can't believe that jury said they weren't."

Grampa's pale face turned pink, and he put both hands flat on the table to keep them steady. "Maybe you didn't know this, son, but in the United States of America, citizens are entitled to a trial by a jury of their peers, and the verdict of the jury stands. It doesn't matter what you or anyone else in that courtroom thought about Bryant and Milam. The jury heard both arguments, considered the evidence, and concluded that those men were innocent. The case is closed, and I don't want to hear another word about it. If you want to keep beating on about that trial, go right ahead, but don't do it around me. It's what your daddy used to do, wear me out about what he thought was right or wrong. Well, Hiram, sometimes boys don't know what's right; sometimes they've got to trust their elders. Twelve adult citizens of the state of Mississippi sat in that courtroom for a full week, and they've given their informed decision."

"But what about—?"

"No buts about it, son. You and I aren't going to talk about this again, and I'd advise you not to talk to anybody around here about it. Our community's suffered enough; it's time for things to get back to normal."

We were mad at each other, so we didn't talk much for the rest of the meal, and by the time Ruthanne cleared the dishes, I was itching to get out of there.

Grampa didn't say anything when I told him I was going for a walk.

The humid night air pressed on me worse than ever; sweat trickled down my back before I'd gotten a block away from home.

It was after nine on a Friday night. A few cars passed as I walked to the bridge, some were packed with kids looking for fun on the first night of a weekend, and seeing them made me wonder what my friends in Tempe were doing, what they'd been doing in the weeks I'd been gone. I was ready to go home, ready to leave Greenwood and Grampa's house, ready to try to patch things up with Dad. About the only thing I'd miss from Greenwood, actually, the only person I'd miss from Greenwood was Naomi.

And I hoped she'd miss me.

I walked down Front Street and cut through the back parking lot of the county courthouse. A few cars were there, probably night-duty police or county jail guards, and except for those, the lot was empty, quiet, and dark. Halfway across, I saw someone, a man it looked like, step out from the shadows behind a Ford sedan parked close to the courthouse's rear entrance.

He flicked a cigarette to the ground when I got closer, and before I could see who he was, he said, "Hey, sisbaby. Where you headed so late at night?" R. C. Rydell stepped out of the shadows, and in the light from the corner streetlight I could see his face was bruised and swollen; blood was splattered down the front of his T-shirt.

I stopped but didn't say anything. He didn't have a knife that I could see.

"Hope you ain't looking for my little sister," he said, "'cause I don't think she's gonna make your little run-dee-voo anytime soon."

"What're you talking about?"

"C'mon, Hiram, you think I'm stupid? What kind of big brother would I be if I didn't know my kid sister had herself a boyfriend?"

"Where is she, R.C.? What happened?"

"Problems at home. Our old man." R.C. lit another cigarette, snapped the match at me, and took a long drag. "Pa really was on one tonight. He's been mean before, but tonight he was crazy, out of control. 'House's a damn pigsty! Kids don't do a damn thing round here! I work all day to keep a roof over our heads and what do I get for it?' That kind of crap. Naomi knows enough to steer clear of him when he's been drinkin' and rantin', and so do I, usually, but tonight he started in on me for being gone, for quittin' my job at the dock and goin' to Jackson."

"You've been in Jackson?"

"No future round here. And believe me, I didn't mind gettin' away from Pa. I got me a job in Jackson loadin' trucks and might start drivin' one in a year or two. I been down there almost a month already. Anyway, Pa don't like it, and he kept yellin', 'Ya run out on me, boy!' What he means is that he couldn't take my wages no more to buy booze. He really tore into me tonight: hollerin', swearin', callin' me all kinds of names. I coulda took it because I knew he was drunk and that after this weekend, I'd be cleared out of here for good, but he pulls out his big old leather belt, starts swingin' it around, swearin', comin' at me." R.C. was breathing hard now, and even in the shadows, I could see the pain on his face.

"He caught me good a couple times and I just took it. That made him mad, so he throws the belt down and starts with his fists." R.C.'s voice got faster. "Hittin' me in the face, kickin' me, screamin' like a crazy man. He popped me in the nose—blood gushed all over, it's probably broke—and that did it. That pulled my trigger, and there was no stoppin' me.

"I whaled on Pa like I was some kind of machine. Hittin' him in the face, left, right, left, poundin' him as hard as I could. He was bleedin' bad, but I kept at him. That's when Naomi started screaming. She tried to make me stop, I don't know, I can't remember very well, but I think she pulled on my arm or somethin', and I shoved her outta the way and kept swingin' at Pa. Pretty soon he went down like a sack of seed, and I started kickin' him, yellin' as loud as I could. I swear, Hiram, I felt like all the hate I'd ever had was pourin' out of me right on to him.

"When he stopped movin', stopped swearin', stopped cryin', I quit, and that's when I could hear Naomi cryin' and beggin' me to leave him alone. She wasn't mad or nothin', but awful scared, maybe scared I'd gone crazy too. I tried talkin' to her, but she was just cryin' and cryin', so I grabbed my duffel bag and got out of there, out for good. I ain't never goin' back. Never."

"You just left Naomi there? What's she going to do?"

"Last I saw her she was bent over Pa, tryin' to clean him up. I told her to leave him be, he had it comin', and she knew it. And you know what? It felt good to rip into my old man. The whole time I was poundin' him, I wanted to kill him. I was honestly trying to beat him to death." He took a deep, shaky pull on his cigarette. "I don't know if I managed it or not, but in case I did, I come down here to let the sheriff know."

"You told the sheriff you beat up your own dad?"

"Sheriff Smith knows all about Pa. He's known what's been goin' on since I was a little kid. Soon as I told him, he said he was surprised it hadn't happened sooner and told me to get on the late bus to Jackson and never come back. Told me he'd take care of Pa and make sure Naomi's okay. You know, for a lawman, Sheriff Smith's all right."

R.C. looked like he'd been through the fight of his life, lost, and was relieved it was finally over. He smiled weakly. "I'm gonna make it in Jackson, Hiram. Things are gonna be different for me."

"Are you sure the sheriff's not doing anything? How do you know he won't come after you?"

"If he does, he does." R.C. shrugged. "I been in trouble with the law before, and I can take it, but like I said, he knows Pa and what's been goin' on at home. He said even if I did kill Pa, he'd consider it self-defense or justifiable homicide or something like that."

"What about all this other stuff?" I asked. "They just had that big trial in Sumner; Bryant and Milam got turned loose."

"He told me about all that and asked me about that nigger trouble that happened last month. Said somebody'd told him I'd been braggin' 'bout how I was goin' to help humble an uppity Northern nigger." He looked at me with a thin smile. "I wonder who woulda done that."

I gulped and took a step back, half expecting R.C. to flatten me. But he just kept talking.

"Anyway, I told him that Bryant and Milam did ask me to help 'em that night, but when I went home after talking to you, Pa was drunk again. Yellin', hittin', same old stuff. That's when I decided I had to get out of here, so I grabbed some things, left home, caught the bus to Jackson, and haven't been back since."

"But I thought—"

"Yeah, you thought I helped kill that Chicago boy. Well, Mr. Sisbaby, I guess I missed my chance." He shrugged his shoulders. "I dunno, I could've done it, but I didn't. Like I said, things are gonna be different for me now. I'm lookin' for a change in Jackson."

"What about Naomi? Where is she? What's she going to do?"

"Naomi's no baby. Livin' with somebody like Pa makes you pretty tough, Hiram Hillburn, so I ain't worried 'bout my kid sister. If Pa's dead, maybe she'll stay in the house a while. Or maybe she'll move in with some do-good neighbor. She can come down to Jackson with me if she wants, but I ain't tellin' her what to do or not to do. She's old enough to figure things out, and I got my own worries."

"Do you know where she is right now? I want to see her, help her if I can."

R.C. took a last long drag on his cigarette, flicked it out into the parking lot, and picked up the duffel bag near his feet. "You didn't hear me, sisbaby. Only thing Pa ever done for her was make her tough, so she don't need your help or nobody else's. She wants to see you, she'll find you. You could go lookin' for her, and maybe you'd find her; she's probably at home or at the hospital if Pa made it, but I doubt she's goin' to be wantin' to see anybody right now. Even you." He touched his nose gingerly, then looked up at the sky for a moment before walking past me. "I gotta get to the bus depot. See you round, sisbaby."

When R.C. left, I walked to the bridge and stood where Naomi and I usually met. I hoped maybe she'd show up later, after she got her dad taken care of. Leaning against the bridge rail, I thought about R. C. Rydell. Was he lying about being in Jackson? Lying about Naomi? R.C. was mean, but I'd never known him to hurt his sister.

But if he was telling the truth, who had been with Bryant and Milam that night they kidnapped Emmett Till? Probably somebody as hateful to Negroes as R.C., but I didn't want to think about it. Like Grampa said, the trial was over, and nobody down here was going to be looking to start another one.

Besides, I wanted to think about Naomi. I'd always known she'd had it bad living with her dad, but until tonight, I really had no idea how rotten things were for her. I didn't know what I could do, but I wanted to be there at the bridge if she decided she needed my help or if she just wanted somebody to talk to. Maybe the best thing for her would be to get out of Greenwood and come back to Arizona with me. She could stay with my family a while, at least until we could find somebody in Tempe for her to live with. My sisters would love her; so would Mom. She could go to Tempe High with me. It'd be hard for her at first, kids would tease her about her Southern accent and stuff, but like R.C. said, Naomi was tough; she could handle whatever Tempe High threw at her.

I sat at the base of that bridge rail for a couple more hours thinking about how great life would be with Naomi in Tempe, figuring out exactly how to convince her to come back with me, aching to see her again, to hold her and let her know that I'd do whatever I could to make things right.

I sat there a long time waiting and dreaming, but she never came. Finally I walked home and went to bed, but I didn't sleep much.

The next morning even the smell of Ruthanne's bacon and biscuits wasn't enough to get me out of bed. I felt flat, wiped out from the trial and everything, sad that my summer was over, and, because I wasn't sure how he'd react, a little worried to go back home and face Dad. I'd be leaving Mississippi in a couple days, and when I got back to Tempe, I'd have to jump right into school and everything else that had started without me. Anyway, I wanted at least one lazy morning in bed before I went back to the grind at home.

I should've been able to sleep in—I felt plenty lazy

enough—but too many things were buzzing in my brain. Not the trial or Emmett Till or R. C. Rydell. That stuff was all done as far as I was concerned. I was worrying about Naomi. Was she all right? Would I see her before I left? If I did, would I be able to talk her into coming to Arizona?

With all that running through my head, I tried to sleep and did doze a little, but I was too restless to sleep soundly, like there was something I should've been doing but wasn't. I was thinking of Naomi too, of course; it would've been impossible not to.

Around 11:00 I heard Grampa talking to somebody down in the driveway below my window. Being lazy had made me bored and hungry, so I decided to get out of bed, get dressed and see what Ruthanne had left me to eat. Before going downstairs I looked out the window and saw Grampa talking to three men I didn't recognize.

Whatever they'd been doing, it looked like they had just about finished up. One man patted Grampa on the shoulder and said, "You just let us worry about this, Mr. Hillburn. We know how to take care of these kinds of things; you can count on us doing it right."

"I hope to get a fair price for it," said Grampa. "It's been good to me all these years."

The man held up a set of keys. "You can't be too choosy about price in this situation, but we'll do what we can. I guarantee you this truck will be out of Mississippi before dark. Soon as we get it sold, you'll get your money."

"I could sell it myself and save a heck of a lot of money

and trouble." Grampa's voice was edgy, like it got when he was mad or tired.

"Sure you could," the man said, "but having it sit around here for too long might end up making more trouble than you want. We'll keep it quiet, and you'll get your money." The man got into the cab and started the truck while his two friends jumped in the back.

Grampa watched them drive away.

When I came downstairs, he was at the kitchen table with a pile of papers spread out in front of him.

"So, the dead rise again," he said with a smile. "Thought you'd never miss one of Ruthanne's breakfasts."

"I decided to sleep in at least once before I have to go back to school." I went to the stove and found a plate of biscuits and jelly Ruthanne had left. I took the plate to the table and sat down across from my grandfather. "Hey, Grampa, what happened to the pickup?"

"I sold the damn thing. It was getting too rattley for me. I'm going to get a car with automatic transmission."

"A car? What are you going to do with a car? Can't haul stuff in it, can't take it out to the plantation. Or fishing. There's not a thing wrong with that old pickup."

"Don't be bothering me about this, Hiram. It's gone, and it's not coming back."

Grampa looked a little mad, and I didn't want to be arguing with him during my last days in Greenwood, but selling that truck made no sense. "I always liked that pickup; there's no good reason for getting rid of it."

"I've got reasons, and I don't have to be explaining them to my grandson." His face got red again, and he started shoving his papers into a big brown envelope. "Adults have reasons for doing what they do, even if they make no sense to children. Children, including *you*, Hiram, have got to learn to trust their elders. That truck's gone, and I don't want to hear any more about it."

"Seems like you don't want to hear any more about anything these days," I snapped back. "First about the trial, then about R.C. or whoever helped Bryant and Milam, and now about the truck."

Grampa ignored me and concentrated on getting his papers into the envelope. There was no sense fighting with him about this; I was going home soon and wouldn't have been driving the truck much anyway, so I cooled off and changed the subject.

"I saw R. C. Rydell last night, Grampa."

He looked up right away. "R. C. Rydell? Did he try to break your neck?"

"We just talked. He was heading out of town after one too many fights with his dad."

"Too bad he's not taking his father with him," Grampa said. "That man's been tormenting his children for longer than should be allowed. It ruined R.C., and I'm sure it was no good for Naomi, even though she seems to have turned out all right. At any rate, she'll be better off with her good-for-nothing brother gone. Where's he headed?"

"Jackson. He's been working down there for almost a

month. And you know something kind of funny? He was down in Jackson the night Bryant and Milam kidnapped Emmett Till. When he first told me that, I thought for sure he was lying, but now I believe him. All this time I thought he was the third man they were looking for, and he wasn't even in the county."

"I wouldn't trust that boy any farther than I could throw him," Grampa said. His voice sounded hurried, nervous. "You can't take anything he says for truth, though I never was convinced he had anything to do with all that trouble with Roy and J.W."

"Well, he's off the hook in case anybody ever starts trying to track down whoever else was in on that killing."

"I told you before, Hiram, no one in the Delta is going to bother with that case again. The jury gave a decision, and the judge accepted it." He got the last of his papers into the envelope and sealed it with the brass clasp. "And now there's no evidence left to link any other person to the kidnapping. As they say, 'This case is closed.'" Grampa smiled, looking more relaxed than he had since before the trial started. "And now it looks like we're going to have to start working on getting you on a train to Arizona."

"Yeah. Do you think you can call Mom and Dad today and let them know the trial's over, and that I'm clear to leave now?"

"News about the trial was in papers all over the country, so I'm sure they know the trial's over, but I'll call and let them know you're coming home as soon as possible. I'd also better have Ruthanne run over to the train depot and make sure we can get you a ticket for tomorrow or Monday."

It surprised me that Grampa was so cheerful about my leaving. Sure, I was anxious to get out of there as fast as I could, but I'd expected him to start with the usual sales pitch to stay in Greenwood. For most of my life he'd been begging me to come back, and now it seemed like he couldn't wait for me to leave.

But I didn't have time to figure him out right then. If I was going to be gone soon, I had to talk to Naomi. I told him I had to go find a friend.

Grampa smiled. "Of course, you have to say good-bye to the girlfriend. Don't be gone too long; you'll need to be getting your things packed up pretty soon." Grampa pushed away from the table and went into the living room, and I headed out the kitchen door for Naomi's house.

When I was walking down the driveway, I spooked Ronnie Remington, who had just come out of his house and was walking his path to the sidewalk with his head down. He almost ran into me when we reached the sidewalk at the same time.

"'Scuse me," he said nervously as he stopped dead in front of me, waiting for me to move out of his way so he could follow his route on the sidewalk. He looked up, and his eyes got wide when he recognized me. "I-I-I'm just going downtown to get some things. I should've been looking where I was going. Ralph's always telling me to look where I'm going, because if I don't, I'm going to run into things or get run over." He gulped and blinked rapidly. "Not that I'm worried about getting run over, or that I'm saying you ever tried to run me over. I'm not saying that at all. No, not at all. You can trust me on that. I did not say that you were driving that old blue Ford pickup with that evil Rydell boy and tried to run me down. I did not say that, and you can rest assured that I will never say that to anyone. Not a single solitary soul." His eyes glazed as he talked faster and faster. "One thing the Hillburns know is that the Remingtons are good neighbors. We never tell anyone anything. Ralph and I, we mind our own business and we trust other people will mind theirs. Your grampa, he knows that. We haven't told a soul about his pickup, not a soul."

I had no idea what he was talking about, so I tried to slow him down. "There's nothing to tell about the pickup, Mr. Remington. Grampa sold it. No secrets there."

"Nobody calls me Mr. Remington." He smiled. "It sounds good, sounds like it should sound. I wonder if I should tell people to start addressing me as Mr. Remington. 'Ronnie' always sounds so childish, and a man at my age, well, Ralph's actually older than I am, so I suppose *he'd* like to be called Mr. Remington too. As a matter of fact, I'm sure he'd like that. We have similar tastes, you know. Well, not about everything, but about some things. A few things, at least. We used to, anyway."

He twitched when I touched his arm to stop him. "Mr. Remington, about the truck. It's . . . no . . . secret," I said slowly. "Grampa sold it is all."

"Of course he sold it. He told us he was going to, after the trial and all and the horrible, horrible trouble that started up in Money. Not that I've even been to Money. Too small. Just a cotton gin and a few stores, I hear. He made Ralph and me promise, as good neighbors, of course, that we wouldn't say anything to anyone about what Ralph saw. Well, when he saw it, he didn't think anything of it at the time. Folks often borrow your grampa's truck, and Ralph of course can't sleep and often watches out the window. Not peeping, of course, of course not that, but in a neighborly way, watching out for our neighbors and their things."

"Ralph saw something?" Something tickled the pit of my stomach.

"Oh no, I promised I would never say that. When your grandfather came over to talk to us about that terrible, terrible tragedy, that Chicago boy they found dead, when he came to talk to us about that, he wanted us to make sure we hadn't seen anything. Well, of course *I* hadn't because I always retire by ten o'clock. If I don't get a good ten hours of sleep, I'm a wreck the next day. So of course I was asleep. But not Ralph. No, Ralph's a night owl. So he saw Roy and J.W. that Saturday night, recognized them right off because he'd gone to high school with J.W., of course, he's a few years older than J.W., but they were in school at the same time. So how could he not recognize them? Ralph remarked to me that he didn't know that your grandfather knew J.W., though. It was that next day he told me that. That about your grandfather and J. W. Milam."

Ronnie's words swirled around my head so fast, I felt dizzy. I wasn't even sure what I was hearing. "Milam? Grampa was with Milam?"

"I never said that. Did I? Promised, Ralph and I, that we wouldn't tell anyone anything about it, and we haven't. We told your grandfather that except for when he told me, Ralph would not ever tell anyone that he'd seen Roy and J.W. drop him off late, oh very late, that night. It was strange, though, for your grandfather to be out so late, and that's probably why Ralph even remembered it. You know he's so forgetful. He drinks, you know. Too much, if you ask me. But will he listen to me? No. Never has, never will. I'm the younger brother, so he thinks he doesn't have to listen to me, even though I'm the only one in the family with any common sense."

The dizziness was getting worse, so I put my hands on Ronnie's shoulders to steady myself and to slow him down. "Please, Mr. Remington, please talk in a straight line, will you?"

That startled him. He paused, looking at my hands on his shoulders, and when I let go, he started talking again, this time more slowly.

"Yes, yes, I do prattle on sometimes. I like it when you call me Mr. Remington. I'm going to have to remember to tell Ralph that. We must have people address us that way."

"About Milam and Bryant. Please?"

"Of course you know about the trial. Ralph and I didn't go, of course, but we read all about it in the *Commonwealth*.

They covered it well, don't you think? Something in there, even nice photos, about the trial every day. Comprehensive coverage, I'd say. Well, we were horrified to read all the details. Such a tragic, tragic thing. And Ralph read about your grandfather's pickup. That one witness, oh what was his name? He saw it Sunday morning, out at that other plantation. Well, I'll never remember his name. That worried Ralph right away, he has such a legal mind, you know. He knew people would know whose truck that was. Circumstantial evidence, of course, of course. It proves very little or nothing, he said. But if it were added to what he saw, you know, Roy and J.W. dropping him off so terribly late one night, and Roy borrowing that truck. Well, pardon the expression, but that would be damning, Ralph said. Quite, quite damning. So of course, we admire your grandfather and his fine work with the Citizens' Councils and all that, and we've always tried to be very good neighbors, so of course when your grandfather came over to chat with us, well, we knew the score. We assured him, as I'm assuring you, that we would never tell anyone anything. Of course, most people don't listen to us anyway. Though I have no idea why."

I felt the blood draining from my face. The dizziness was back, and the breakfast I'd just eaten felt like rocks in my stomach.

"My, Hiram, you don't look so well. You know, this Indian summer we're having is quite brutal. The heat, over ninety hasn't it been, with all this humidity, well it is, of course, the South, but it's just brutal. You should get right back inside, out of this sun, and have yourself a nice cold glass of iced tea."

I moved off the sidewalk, and as soon as the way was clear, Ronnie moved past me, still talking as he walked. "Iced tea. That will help. Yes, it would. Of course with sugar and a slice of lemon . . ."

The sun did feel brutal. The air close, damp, and heavy; so thick, I could hardly breathe. Had I even been breathing? It felt like Ronnie sucked up all the air when he talked, so fast, so much, and what he said. The weight of his words and the weather and everything else from that Mississippi summer squeezed all the air out of me. I half staggered back into the house.

Grampa was reading in the living room when I came in and flopped onto the sofa, but I didn't even look at him. With my head still spinning, I leaned back and stared at the ceiling, waiting for the dizziness to pass. I could feel my grandfather's presence in the room but he said nothing. He was watching me, waiting. Maybe worried. Would he still worry about me?

Or was he worried about himself?

My head cleared enough that I could sit up. Grampa was in his chair, and he smiled at me. "Are you feeling all right, son?" He looked concerned, looked just like my grandfather had always looked. His voice sounded soothing, like I was back home. The sights, sounds, and smells of Gramma's house. Those were all around me. Cozy. It felt good.

Then I remembered Ronnie. Had it been a dream? Had I even seen him? Maybe it was all some sort of hallucination.

I looked at Grampa. I loved him. I knew he loved me. We were both sitting in a room where we'd read together, listened to the radio, where he'd played with me when I was a little boy. This room, this house, this man were all a part of my roots, all parts of a memory I had always loved.

But another, newer memory nagged my conscience. I tried to ignore it. I wanted to forget it, but the Hillburn stubbornness wouldn't let me. I knew I could settle it with one statement, not even a question. I could say it, watch my grandfather and know. I'd know immediately, know if my roots were solid as ever or if they'd withered and rotted.

I looked at Grampa, his face full of concern and love for me. I felt his love. I loved him, I had always loved him.

"Grampa, Ronnie Remington told me something about a promise."

He didn't move. His expression didn't change. His look of concern stayed the same. But his eyes, his eyes looked desperate when he shook his head, chuckled, and said, "Oh, that Ronnie Remington, he talks in such circles that he could drown a man."

"You were there. That night, you were there."

My grandfather's smile faded. He looked away from me and whispered, "The boy was alive when I left; they promised they were done with him when they brought me home."

And then I knew.

Knew what I didn't want to know.

CHAPTER 17

On my last Sunday in Greenwood, I slept late, waiting for my grandfather to get up and eat breakfast and find something to do before I came downstairs. By 11:00 I was up and dressed, and, without seeing my grandfather, went looking for Naomi. I had to talk to her before I left Mississippi; I needed to talk to someone, someone I cared about and could trust.

I made it to our place on the bridge before noon. By then most people had finished their church meetings, and some, still in their Sunday best, were out for a walk. The heat wave had broken Saturday night, and citizens of Greenwood were in their yards and on the streets savoring the first day of fall-like weather.

Naomi wasn't at our spot at the center of the bridge, so I walked across hoping to see her somewhere along the way.

For half an hour I hung around on the north end watching little kids kick rocks into the yellow-green water of the Yazoo when their mothers weren't looking.

Naomi never showed up, so I walked back over the bridge and headed down River Road to her house. When I crossed the highway at the edge of town, the pavement turned to gravel, and I crunched along about a mile past the cotton gin until I came to the Rydells' beat-up shack. It looked deserted: trees and bushes grew thick in the property behind her house, and long grass and weeds filled the front yard. Most of the paint on the clapboard siding had peeled off long before, and the sagging roof over the porch looked ready to cave in with the next strong wind. The porch steps creaked when I climbed up to the front door. I knocked and waited. Nothing. I knocked again, harder. "Naomi? Hey, Naomi, it's Hiram." Still nothing. I pounded again. "Naomi! Are you in there?" Something, a squirrel probably, rustled behind the house, but nothing else moved. I walked through the weeds all the way around the house, hoping to see some sign of her or maybe to find a note she'd left for me.

Nobody was home, and nobody'd been expecting me to stop by.

Feeling hurt and empty, I headed back into town, hoping R.C. was right, that Naomi could and would take care of herself.

For the rest of that day my grandfather and I avoided each other. I didn't come home until supper time, and by then he was back in his bedroom.

"Your granddaddy don't feel well, Mr. Hiram," Ruthanne said when I walked into the kitchen for supper, "and wants you to go on ahead and eat without him." She set the food on the table. "That trial laid him low, lower than I'd a thought it would. Could be old Mr. Hillburn's finally having a change of heart. If that be the case—and if it's catching—maybe something good might come out of Emmett's death after all. All that grief and suffering that boy's poor mama's been through, Lord, I hope it ain't all in vain."

She looked sad for a moment, then she remembered what she was doing and motioned for me to sit at the table. "Don't know how long it'll be before you come back this way, Mr. Hiram, so I've made all your favorite Southern foods, and I expect you to eat up. Every bite. I don't want your mama complaining that you come home looking skinny."

For some reason I was starving, and I piled my plate with fried chicken, biscuits, mashed potatoes and gravy, string beans, okra. When I got through that, Ruthanne brought out a slab of ham lacquered with honey glaze. Sweet potatoes. Warm spiced applesauce and coleslaw. I ate while Ruthanne made small talk about her children and their comings and goings. She sure loved her kids. I hoped they knew how lucky they were to have a mother like her.

When my fork clattered on the empty plate, she told me to go take a walk—"Maybe you'll run into that little Rydell girl"—and to come back ready for pie: gooseberry, rhubarb, and sweet potato. "If you find your friend while you're out making room for dessert, tell her she's surely welcome to set here and share our pie; we've got plenty."

I wandered the streets of Greenwood for about an hour, came back, alone, and had some pie. Before I went upstairs to bed, I thanked Ruthanne for everything she'd done for me.

Monday, my last day in Mississippi.

At breakfast, Ruthanne said, "Your granddaddy ate while you were upstairs packing. After that, somebody picked him up and took him down to the courthouse and from there to go look for a car. He's gonna be busy, but he promised he'll be back before your train leaves. Feels bad he can't make it to the station, but he wants to say good-bye to you 'fore you go." She looked at me carefully. "Mr. Hiram, are things all right with you and Mr. Hillburn? You both seem awful skittish of each other."

What could I say? What could I tell *her*?

"I guess that trial just took a lot out of him," I said without looking up from my plate. "He hasn't been the same since."

Ruthanne waited for me to say more, but I concentrated on the food in front of me. She watched me eat for a moment, and then she turned, shaking her head.

After breakfast I walked to the courthouse to see Sheriff Smith; when I got to his office, his secretary sent me right in.

The sheriff looked up from his desk. "Hiram Hillburn, I figured you'd be back in Arizona by now. You ain't planning on staying permanent in Greenwood, are you?"

"Nosir. I'm leaving this afternoon. If it's okay, though, I wanted to ask you a few things before I leave."

He leaned back in his chair and stretched. "Fire away."

"Well, about Naomi Rydell. I ran into R.C. the other night—"

"You know," he interrupted, "I finally did talk to R.C. about his involvement with the trouble up in Money. The boy had an airtight alibi."

"I know."

"Really? Well, I just wanted to make sure you knew that we took your call seriously. Now, what about his sister?"

"R.C. told me about his dad and everything, and I was wondering, well, what's happened to Mr. Rydell?"

"Not dead, unfortunately. He got busted up bad, but not bad enough. He'll be in the hospital a good while."

"What about Naomi?"

"She told me you might be asking." The sheriff smiled. "Nice girl, Naomi Rydell, and it's a miracle she survived that home she's been raised in. I suppose I should have done something sooner, but the law's pretty soft on fathers, especially when there's no mother. Heck, Naomi was mother and father both for that house since she was eight years old. But you're wondering where she is. Let's just say she's in a safe place. We found her a good home, somewhere her father won't be able to hurt her again, where she can enjoy the last couple years of her childhood."

"If she knew I'd be looking, did she say anything, leave me a note or something?"

He shook his head. "Things happened fast after R.C. licked their daddy. Naomi was pretty upset and didn't have time to do much letter-writing." He stood and reached his hand across the desk. "But I will tell her you came by."

Mr. Paul had a couple of customers when I got to his stand in the courthouse lobby, so I hung back, waiting until they were gone. "Hey, Mr. Paul," I said when they'd left.

"Hiram Hillburn, I figured you'd be long gone by now. Don't you have to be getting back to school?"

"I'm leaving this afternoon, but I wanted to come over and say good-bye."

"That's thoughtful of you. So, are you glad you came to Greenwood?"

"I don't know. Sometimes I am, and sometimes I'm not."

"My guess is that sitting through the trial won't be one of your summer highlights."

"I didn't like the trial or any of the stuff that happened before it, but you know what was the worst of all? It was knowing that everybody in that courtroom knew Emmett Till had been murdered; some probably even had something to do with it. And that jury sat there for a week, listening to evidence and testimony so clear that even my little brothers could've figured it out, and they go and give a not guilty verdict."

"Least they had a trial," Mr. Paul said.

"But the trial didn't make any difference. These guys got away with murder anyway."

"Sure the boys got off, but you can't tell me the next peckerwood who's got lynching on his mind isn't going to worry just a little that he might end up in a courtroom."

"What about the people who don't get caught? The people who never go to trial? They get away with murder too."

"In a way they do, but they've also got to live with it the rest of their lives. Can you imagine always worrying about getting caught? About someone finding out?"

"Yeah, but it's hard knowing that people can hide so much badness inside themselves, people you think you know and love. It makes you wonder about everybody."

"Folks sometimes do ugly things, Hiram, but that don't necessarily make them evil. A lot of good folks just make stupid decisions or get themselves in the wrong place at the wrong time."

"But even if he's in the wrong place at the wrong time, a good person shouldn't go along. He should leave or stop whatever bad that's happening."

"Sure he should. Sure should all of us." Mr. Paul paused. "Have *you* always managed that?"

That gave me something to think about while I walked home.

When I got back to my grandfather's house, a new Chevy sedan sat in the driveway.

"Got that automatic transmission," my grandfather said when I came into the living room. "And got a good deal on it." He motioned for me to sit down. "Where've you been, son?"

I kept standing. I still didn't feel like talking to him long. "Around town. Saying good-bye to some people."

"What time's your train leave?"

"Two o'clock. I guess Ruthanne's going to take me?"

"In that new Chevy. But she's expecting to feed you lunch before you go. It's her last chance to fatten you up before you leave Mississippi." He grinned. Like old times.

I stood there a moment without saying anything. Then I said, "I guess I better get my bags in the car. Smells like lunch is about ready."

When I came back into the house, my grandfather was already at the table.

"Mr. Hiram," Ruthanne said, "I do hope you've saved yourself a little appetite. You're going to hurt my feelings if you don't clean up all this food before you go."

"Ruthanne," my grandfather said, "I'm sure that between the two of us, we can make a good dent in this splendid meal, but whatever we don't eat, you can send with him on the train."

"Could, but I've already packed him a little something for the trip." She pointed to a large grocery bag on the counter. "Don't want to weigh him down with too many things. Ya'll get busy eating," she said as she set a bowl of potato salad on the table. "I'll be upstairs, Mr. Hiram, so you just give me a holler when you're ready to go to the station."

When Ruthanne left, my grandfather said, "Son, I'm sure going to miss having you around the house." His voice sounded soft and tired. "For a while it seemed like the old days when you were little, and Gramma was still here. You know, I still miss her, miss her terribly, and it's going to be pretty hard getting used to an empty house again." His eyes got watery. "It was so wonderful having you here. I only wish . . . I wish there hadn't been so many distractions. It wasn't fair for you to get caught up in that trial business."

"Maybe, but it taught me some things." I stared at him, wondering what he'd say.

He held my stare a moment, and then looked down. "About that, Hiram, you know I tried everything I could to keep you away from that trial. There was no need for you to get involved."

"It was the right thing to do," I said. "When I left home, I promised Mom I'd do what was right, and at the time, I figured I knew something that might have made a difference in the trial. That's why I told the sheriff, even though I didn't want to. That's why I went to the trial, even though I didn't want to. Turns out that what I knew didn't have a thing to do with the kidnapping and murder of Emmett Till." I waited for my grandfather to say something. To apologize. Wouldn't he want to clear his conscience, at least with me, before I left?

"Well," he said, "the trial took a different direction, didn't it? Apparently the prosecution had decided either that Mose Wright's testimony was faulty or there wasn't sufficient evidence that others had helped Bryant and Milam do anything. And, of course, the jury wasn't convinced that Bryant and Milam did anything at all to that Till boy. I'm sure there will be rumors floating around for a while—there always are after a sensational trial—but soon enough those will die down and things will get back to normal. What you need to remember, son"—Grampa narrowed his eyes—"is that you can't believe everything you hear. Nothing's as simple as you might think."

That was the last either of us talked about the trial. For the rest of lunch we talked about my brothers and sisters, about life in Tempe, about the weather, his crops, and anything except his guilt. When the time came for me to leave, we said good-bye and hugged. Grampa got teary-eyed as I carried the rest of my things out the front door to the car.

All the way to the station I tried to convince Ruthanne that she didn't have to wait with me. We were standing behind my grandfather's new Chevy, and I had my bags in hand when she finally agreed.

"You sure, now? I don't want you getting on the wrong train and ending up in New York or someplace worse."

"Ruthanne, I'm sixteen. Only one train's passing through here in the next two hours. I'm sure I can figure it out."

She looked a little sad. "Well, I'm going to miss you around the house. Never did see anything brighten up your granddaddy like having you here did." She tucked the grocery bag she had packed for me under my arm. "Now, you be careful on that train, and don't you dare share this with any strangers. You take care, Mr. Hiram, and be sure to say my hello to your mama and daddy."

Except for the stationmaster who checked my ticket and

a couple of railroad workers, the station was empty, and I wished I had a book or magazine to read while I waited for my train. I set my bags on a wooden slat bench on the platform and was ready to walk to a drugstore on Carrollton Avenue to pick something up when I saw her.

It didn't look like Naomi at first. She was wearing a bright new cotton dress, and her blonde hair was brushed out, down to her shoulders. But maybe the biggest difference was that she didn't look so defeated.

She walked right to me, took my hand, and sat down on the bench. "I'm glad I got here before you left, Hiram. I've been wanting to talk to you . . . but, well, things got complicated pretty fast." Her hand felt warm, relaxed. She told me Sheriff Smith had found her a family to live with, a good family who'd take care of her; she'd finish high school, and then maybe go to secretarial school or even college. Naomi sounded full of hope.

We sat on that bench and talked until my train came. When we hugged good-bye, I felt her tears on my cheek. "I hope you come back someday, Hiram," she whispered. "Things, everything, will be better then."

I couldn't answer because if I did, I knew I'd cry. I just hugged her tighter and prayed nothing but good would come her way for the rest of her life. She'd already had a lifetime share of the bad.

The train whistled twice, and a conductor called, "All aboard!" I stood up and grabbed my bags. "Thanks, Naomi," I said. "Thanks for everything."

I got on the train just before it started moving, and from my window seat, I watched Naomi standing alone on the platform until the train was out of sight.

Naomi was all right, was going to be all right. It was nice leaving Greenwood knowing that.

When I got back to Arizona, Dad, not Mom, met me at the station in Phoenix. That surprised me. Dad was always busy with something, stuff at work or church or with the little kids, so Mom usually had to deal with me.

Then I remembered that he'd probably followed every minute of the trial, not because I might have been in it, but because it was about somebody like Emmett Till getting killed in Mississippi. Of course he'd follow a civil rights case, especially when it was in Mississippi, and he probably couldn't wait to get my eyewitness account of the whole trial. Fine. If he wanted to know about the trial, I'd tell him— tell him almost everything.

When I stepped off the train, he was alone, looking over the crowd trying to spot me. He didn't see me at first and I didn't wave or call to him, I just watched. He looked a little like my grandfather, not as heavy, but his face, the way his hair was graying, even the way he moved. At least in appearance, he definitely was his father's son. After a minute or so, the crowd thinned enough for him to see me. He smiled, waved, and walked over to me.

"Welcome home, son," he said. We shook hands, and then he reached out and put a hand on my shoulder. "We've missed you."

Dad and I stood facing each other awkwardly for a moment. I was almost as tall as he was. He looked a little older, tireder. For a second, our eyes met, and something passed between us, an understanding of some sort, from one Mississippi boy to another.

Then Dad patted my shoulder and picked up my bags; I followed him out to the parking lot.

It's a good ten miles from the Phoenix train depot to our house in Tempe. Even in late September the weather was still hot, and Dad had all the car windows down as we headed home. The dry air swirled through the station wagon moving things around but not really cooling us off. For the first few minutes neither one of us said anything, but I wanted to at least try to talk to Dad to see if we could talk without ending up in a fight.

"How's everybody?" I asked.

"Better, now that school's started. The kids were getting pretty antsy the last couple weeks of summer. Too much time on their hands was not a good thing." Dad cleared his throat, and while keeping his eyes on the road, said, "That trial, it really must have been something. I kept thinking of that poor boy's mother, of his entire family, how awful it must have been for them to see and hear all that evidence and then to have that jury turn Bryant and Milam loose." He sighed. "It's been like that for too long down there, but maybe all the attention that trial got will put people on warning. Desegregation was already on its way, and then the trial. I can imagine how my dad's taking it. Of course, nothing in the Delta's going to change any time soon, but it's a start, a step in the right direction." He glanced at me as if he'd just remembered something and said, "Sorry, Hiram. Probably the last thing in the world you want to think about right now is that trial. Tell me about Greenwood. Are you glad you went?"

"Sort of. Greenwood was exactly how I remembered it. The town and the house haven't changed a bit. When I first got there, I thought I'd never want to leave; then stuff started happening, ugly kinds of stuff."

"The trial?" asked Dad.

"And other things. Some people there were terrific, but a lot of them, I don't know, they seemed to have a meanness in them. They were friendly and all that, but . . ."

"They weren't very nice to Negroes."

"Yeah, but it took me a while to notice that. I guess when I was a little kid, that was all going on over my head. At least it never registered with me."

"And what about Grampa?"

"For a while it was like the old days when he and Gramma were taking care of me. We went fishing, went out to the fields, ate at the Riverside Café. It was a lot of fun." Then I wondered something. "Dad, did you ever do stuff like that with him?"

"All the time. Being the only child, I was pretty spoiled."

"When did it change?"

"Dad never did change; he always wanted to do things with me, but gradually I stopped wanting to do things with him. I guess in a way, it was kind of like it was for you. I got older and started noticing some things I hadn't noticed before. When I saw things I didn't like, I wouldn't shut up about them, and Dad didn't like that at all. Any time I'd want to argue, he'd just tell me, 'Children've got to learn to trust their elders,' and figure that would shut me up. It did for a while, but when I got old enough to start thinking for myself, I learned that kids can't always trust everything their elders do. And that was the beginning of the end for me and Dad."

"Did you stop loving him?" I asked.

"For a long time I thought I did, but then I realized that no matter how wrong or bad or stubborn your father is, he's still your father. I sure didn't like the things he did and said, and frankly, lots of times I didn't like *him,* but he's my father, and he loved me, and for that I love him." He glanced over at me. "What about you?"

I didn't answer right away. Maybe I wouldn't be able to answer for a long time. I knew some things, some horrible things, about my grandfather. Dad probably did too. "I don't know. Grampa's pretty complicated. I guess I'm still working on it."

Dad reached over and patted my leg. He looked a little embarrassed. "I wasn't asking about Grampa."

HISTORICAL NOTE

While visiting his uncle in Money, Mississippi, in August 1955, Emmett Till, a fourteen-year-old African American boy from Chicago, was kidnapped and murdered for allegedly whistling at a white woman in the Bryant's Grocery and Meat Market.

Two men, Roy Bryant and his half brother J. W. Milam, were arrested and tried for the murder but were acquitted by an all-white jury after a brief trial that received intense national and international attention. In an interview published in *Look* magazine three months after their acquittal, Bryant and Milam described how they had kidnapped, tortured, and finally murdered Emmett Till. Milam died in 1983, Bryant in 1994. The third white man and the white woman involved in the kidnapping and subsequent events were never identified or apprehended.

This novel is a work of historical fiction. Though Hiram Hillburn, R. C. Rydell, and many other characters in this story never existed, the events directly related to Emmett Till's kidnapping, murder, and the trial of his killers are true, and the material from *The Greenwood Commonwealth* is presented as it actually appeared in 1955.